EXILE

A MERCY NOVEL

ALSO BY

MERCY

EXILE

A MERCY NOVEL

Rebecca Lim

HYPERION

NEW YORK

First U.S. edition, 2013
First published in Australia in 2011 by HarperCollins Publishers
Australia Pty Limited
1 3 5 7 9 10 8 6 4 2
G475-5664-5-13046

Library of Congress Cataloging-in-Publication Data
Lim, Rebecca.
Exile: a Mercy novel/Rebecca Lim.—1st U.S. ed.
p. cm.
Summary: Exiled angel Mercy "wakes" as unhappy teen Lela, who cares for
her dying mother but never herself, and as Mercy begins to remember Ryan, the
boy she fell in love with in another life, and Luc, the angel haunting her dreams,
she must decide whether to risk Lela's life to gain her heart's desire.
ISBN 978-1-4231-4520-2 (hardback)
[1. Angels—Fiction. 2. Supernatural—Fiction. 3. Caregivers—Fiction.
4. Death—Fiction. 5. High schools—Fiction. 6. Schools—Fiction.] I. Title.
PZ7.L6342Exi 2013
[Fic]—dc23   2012041669

Text set in 12-point Sabon
Designed by Marci Senders

Reinforced binding

Visit www.un-requiredreading.com

THIS LABEL APPLIES TO TEXT STOCK

To my father, Yean Kai, my mother, Susan,
and to Ruth and Eugenia,
with love

AND IF I DIE BEFORE I LEARN TO SPEAK

CAN MONEY PAY FOR ALL THE DAYS I LIVED AWAKE

BUT HALF ASLEEP?

—*PRIMITIVE RADIO GODS*

1

I'm alone in the infinite darkness, the endless vacuum of space. There's nothing to give form to the place I occupy—no up, no down, no sense of distance—nothing except the bright white light coming off my skin.

I am weightless. My feet don't touch the ground. There *is* no ground. Just a breathless, waiting void.

Then, as I watch, I see another light—like me?—wink into being. And another, and another, until all around there are hundreds of lights—no, upwards of a thousand—scattered across the abyss. Like fireflies, like diamonds. All waiting.

And then a giant breath sweeps through us, past us, lifting my hair, ruffling the edges of my drifting garments.

Be, it seems to say. *Live.*

And as I watch, planets, stars, suns, moons explode into being, in every color, in every shade, as if rendered by a painter's hand. Greater and lesser bodies fly by. Comets, black holes, supernovae, strange fissures in time and space twist and curl overhead like a painted, yet living, ever-changing dome.

And I know where I am, and my shining form seems to grow brighter, as do all the others like me out there. Our hearts swelling.

We're home.

Home.

It must be over, over at last.

No more fear, no more uncertainty.

I'm free.

And my sudden joy is so fierce that it seems more than I can contain. I lift my hands to my face in awe, in praise, and feel tears spring to my eyes, feel them course freely down my cheeks.

And that's when I realize that something is wrong.

Because I cannot cry. Was not formed to cry tears.

Only humans cry tears, and I'm not human, am I?

This is a dream.

Instantly, everything vanishes and it's dark again,

bitterly dark. But I'm not alone this time.

"Hello, my love," he says, the two of us soaring toward each other, ghostly, in the void.

Luc.

My beloved.

The most beautiful being in creation. Golden-skinned, golden-haired, broad-shouldered, snake-hipped, long and lean. With eyes as pale as living ice, like broken water. He's heart-stopping.

Even now, in my dream, when I look at him and then look at me, I can't understand how we were together, what he saw in me in the first place.

Luc places his hands around my waist and turns me about in the weightless dark, the better to see me, to see my face.

As I cry, "Where have you been? Why won't you save me? I've been so lost," I am disgusted at myself for saying the words, for acting like a clingy girlfriend when I never was before.

In answer, he laughs and pulls me close and rests his chin atop my hair, the gesture so familiar, so longed for, that I close my eyes and let the tears fall and keep falling.

"Don't do this to me," I sob. "Don't show me the

things I can't have. I want to go home. I want things to be the way they used to be."

"I can't save you," he answers gently, cupping my face with his hands. "Only you can do that. And I can't restart the clock—that time is over and everything has changed and cannot be remade. But I can help you. This time I know I can help you. But you have to do one thing for me."

I'm instantly still in his arms, listening.

His voice is low and urgent, as if he fears being overheard. "The Eight have made it impossible for me to find you. They shift you again and again, into an unbroken chain of strangers—geography, culture, language, all of it random, without pattern. Many times I've almost caught up with you, but then They've cast you into some new form among the billions that teem upon the earth—and so the chase begins again. It's why I am only ever able to reach you in your sleep, in your dreams—where I beg for you to find *me*. But you never have."

He laughs, but I feel his towering frustration.

"It's not your fault," he says. "I don't blame you. They've corrupted you, made you less than you are. But now you need to try to remember something—do you think you can do that?"

His arms tighten around me, and it feels as if I am touching eternity, touching absolute power. Though what is truly at the heart of Luc is walled off from me, as it always was. He's beautiful, yes. Dearer to me than life itself, undoubtedly. But he's always been unknowable. A mystery.

He puts a finger to my lips before I can say anything.

"I almost caught up with you the last time, did you know that? When you were Carmen Zappacosta."

When he says the name, the blank void around us lights up for an instant with a blinding flash—brighter than magnesium when it burns, than lightning come down to earth—and I cringe.

Then the dark surrounds us once more, and he whispers, "I was so close that I almost placed my hands on you through that girl's skin. We were almost together again. In the same place. After all this time."

I shiver at the implication.

"I don't remember being . . . her," I whisper, fearful of the heavens bursting into flame around us if I utter the girl's name.

"They don't want you to remember," he replies, tightening his arms around me. "That's why I'm here. Before They shifted you out of her body, I saw a way for us to be together again. I saw the boy's eyes when he looked at Carmen—it was love for *you* in them. He knows you and loves you for yourself, and that is something we may use to our advantage. I have found a way to free you at last, for us to be together again."

I stare at Luc, confusion on my face. Someone else loves . . . *me*?

"Remember this," Luc urges. "Just this thought. When you wake, I want you to find Ryan Daley and return to Paradise, the place where he lives, and wait for me there. Do you think you can do that?"

"Ryan Daley?" I repeat, relieved when the universe does not burn at the mention of the name.

Luc nods. "I may be prevented from finding you, but you're strong, you're resourceful—you've survived this long without losing your mind. Find the boy, escape the Eight, and return to the godforsaken place he calls home. There we shall be reunited at last. When you are under my protection once more, the Eight will never touch you again."

I stare up at Luc, wondering why he is asking me to find some human boy that I can't even remember.

"Who is he?" I ask. "How will I know him?"

Something flares in Luc's pale eyes for a split second as he gazes at me, his fingers tightening on my waist like talons. For a moment, I'm almost afraid. When he looks like that, he's capable of . . . anything.

Then he laughs, and this time there's genuine amusement there. "As to who he is? I will leave it up to you to find out. You're a smart girl, you'll manage it. As to what he looks like . . ."

Luc propels himself away from me, up into the airless void, turning and turning with his arms outstretched until he is a shining blur, then a pinpoint of light that suddenly vanishes from view. And before me stands his human double, wearing a beat-up leather jacket, a faded navy T-shirt, blue jeans, and scuffed boots. Physically, he's everything Luc is: tall, lean, beautiful, strong. But dark-haired, dark-eyed, fair-skinned, as night is to day. And mortal.

There's something vulnerable in his expression, something Luc has never been and never will be. And then I see it, too. There's love in the boy's eyes. *For me.*

I shift closer to the tall, achingly familiar young man, incredulous that I could have forgotten someone so beautiful; someone who so obviously adores me even though he can't ever have actually seen me, the real me.

Ryan moves closer, too, our fingertips meeting between us.

Something feels as if it is giving way inside me. As if buried memories are struggling to the surface; as if the ground is shifting beneath my feet.

Except there *is* no ground, no up, no down. No light, save for the illumination that's burning off my skin, that's bleeding from me in little drifts, in errant curls of pure energy.

And suddenly I'm alone again, except for Luc's voice, which seems to be coming from everywhere and nowhere all at once.

"Find him." The words reverberate in the impenetrable dark. "Find him and wait for my return."

2

"Lela? Lela, darling? You've fallen asleep in the chair again, honey. If you don't hurry, you're going to be late for work."

I frown, and the last remnants of my dream—vivid, hyperreal—flee and do not return, although I try to hold on to them.

Even before I open my eyes I can smell eucalyptus oil and sandalwood incense, but the intense aroma is unable to mask the smell of sickness in the overheated room: the odor of charred flesh; a chemical residue that is offensive to my senses. There's the whir of a machine, also; a type of medicated inhalant in the air.

Even before I open my eyes, it's obvious to me that some kind of alchemy has taken place again. I've been pulled out of wherever I was before, the life I was living, the body I was in, and dumped into . . . Lela's.

But my real name is not Lela.

It's not even Mercy, which is the name I've given myself in the absence of the real thing. I have no name and no memory. Or rather, there are holes in my memory you could sail a cruise ship through. There's no logic to the way my mind works, nothing ever seems to line up. Like how I know that I know Latin, but I can't ever recall learning it. And how I hate being touched—it's something instinctive in me; I'm big on personal space, on the whole *live and let live* thing, but—right now?—I couldn't tell you why.

The world that I move through seems always like a vacuum to me: I can't recall the specifics of its contours— its geographical boundaries—the languages and customs of its people, yet I know that I can handle myself anytime, anywhere; that I'm fast and I will always hit the ground running, because I have to.

But if I think hard about myself, really hard, I get that one word. *Mercy.* So it's what I call myself, for want of something better. Because if you have a name, you must exist, right? It's something I tell myself a lot.

I open my eyes and see a woman lying in a double bed in front of my armchair. She has sallow, shiny skin, deep lines running between her mouth and nose, dark circles beneath her dark blue eyes, the whites of which are the palest yellow in color, and a cheerful scarf tied tightly around her bald head.

Cancer, whispers my inner voice immediately. *Chemotherapy. Radiation.*

I look across the room at the tri-fold mirror on top of the battered dressing table and see three reflections staring back, though there are only two people physically in the room. I'm unable to suppress the chill flash that races across my skin as I take stock of the third face—which has no connection to Lela, or to the woman in the bed.

It's *my* face. Oval in shape, with brown eyes, pale skin, a mouth with lips that are neither too thin nor too wide; a long, straight nose. It's a ghost's face, a palimpsest of a face, framed by shoulder-length brown hair, each strand straight, even, and perfectly the same, without flaws, without highlights.

I'm taller than she is, than Lela. Broad through the shoulders. Long limbs. Stern face.

Lela is almost the physical opposite of me: petite, but with a womanly figure, curves where there should be curves. Her baggy red plaid pajamas can't hide that. Her thick, red-brown hair is clean and unruly and cut in a choppy bob. She has navy blue eyes and fine, Irish skin; uneven teeth, elegant ankles, trim wrists, tiny hands and feet. A friendly face, I decide. A friendly looking person. Pleasant; no great beauty.

"I'm sorry I woke you," the woman says, and sighs against her pillows. "But you said you can't afford to upset Mr. Dymovsky again, and if you don't get the 7:08 bus you're not going to make it. That's what you told me."

"It's all right, Mum," I say without hesitation. If the woman beneath the bedcovers were not so thin and ill, prematurely aged and drawn, she and Lela would be the image of each other, save thirty years.

I stand and bend over her, give her the briefest of kisses on her paper-dry cheek, wrinkling my nose at the burnt-flesh-chemical smell of her. I twitch straight her garishly bright head scarf, pull the bedclothes up over her brittle collarbones. All of these actions are Lela's impulses, done before I realize I'm doing them. Lela loves her mother, and some things, I've found, the body simply remembers.

"Thank you, sweetheart," the woman whispers. "Now go. Remember to eat. I'll be fine. Georgia will be here for her usual shift, and Bernadette's coming in the afternoon to do some cleaning and help bathe me. I've got the pump, and I'm as comfortable as can be expected. Father Davey phoned to say he'll pop in, though goodness knows why. I'm not at death's door." She gives me a ghost of a smile.

She is, though. Both she and I know it.

She closes her pain-shadowed eyes. "I'll see you after five, darling bud. Love my girl."

I pause, sorry to draw her back to me, but I have no idea where to start living Lela's life, how to walk purposefully out into Lela's day.

"If I wanted to call him, Mum," I say, shaking her gently by the shoulder, "where would I find his card?"

She frowns weakly, no energy left even to open her eyes. "Card?" she murmurs. "What card?"

"Mr. Dymovsky's card," I reply, the syllables awkward on my tongue. "I should call ahead. He won't be so angry if I call ahead."

She's silent for so long, I wonder if she's fallen asleep. Perhaps I'll have to get the answer I want some other way. I glance out the door into the dim hallway of this stranger's house and wonder how many rooms there are, and whether the information would even be here in physical form. Maybe it's just inside Lela's head. The place is a mess. There's dust on almost every surface, and I sense that the older woman's illness has stopped time in this house. Nothing is more important than making sure she is comfortable; keeping vigil over her life.

I know the woman is dying, that the treatments have failed. Not only can I detect the sickness in her, I smell the medication seeping out of her pores. There's no part of her body that does not carry the taint of both, comingled.

I wonder if Lela knows how serious it is. If she truly understands.

When the woman at last replies, her voice is very quiet. "I don't know about any card, love, but it's in the book."

She coughs and keeps coughing for several minutes.

Once she's still, I say with genuine puzzlement, "What book?"

A tiny crease appears between her closed eyes. "The phone book, Lela. The Green Lantern's in the phone book, isn't it? And it's in the kitchen, where it's always been, unless you've gone and moved it. Tell Reggie to tell Mr. Dymovsky, if you don't want to speak to him yourself. You've stood up for *her* often enough, Lord knows why. . . ."

For a while, I watch the shallow rise and fall of the woman's chest as her breathing evens out into sleep.

Time to get this show on the road, I tell myself grimly, wishing I, too, were still asleep, wishing that the dream I can no longer recall would go on forever, taking me with it.

Lela's eyes meet mine in the dresser mirror as I place her feet into the worn slippers beside the armchair.

It's 7:27 by the time I leave the house with Lela's backpack over one shoulder, her bus pass clutched in one hand. The bus stop is less than one hundred yards from the house; I see a bus pulling away as I walk up to it.

There are two people standing there, both isolated from me by their audio equipment. One is a tall, voluptuous, heavy-eyed woman in sweatpants and a loose white blouse, her mass of wavy dark brown hair caught up in a tight, messy ponytail, her feet in a pair of cheap flip-flops, a black leather handbag slung over one shoulder. She's young, and her face is free of makeup, but there's an expression on it that's hard, or wary, and makes her look far older than she really is. Inside her shapeless getup she's practically slouching to make herself seem even more shapeless. What's that word men use to praise and objectify? That's right, *hourglass*. She has an hourglass figure, killer curves under there.

The other is a male—late teens? early twenties?—with sandy dreadlocks pulled back into a thick ponytail. He's wearing a washed-out band T-shirt and long shorts, a stained messenger bag slung across his body, the reflector strip across the bottom grimy in the daylight; one hand on the edge of a skateboard. He checks me out quite openly as I walk toward him, only looking away hastily when he appears to recognize who I am. It's clear he's seen Lela before; I can tell from the complicated expression on his face. He must live in one of the houses nearby. See her around, and often.

I guess I move differently from the way Lela usually does. And I'm dressed like a car crash—in a bright green tank top with rhinestones spelling out the word *Starlet*, a floral skirt scattered with big red splashy blooms, and red flat shoes. It was the only vaguely matching full outfit I could pull together quickly in Lela's messy bedroom. Clothing was spilling out of her battered, old, two-door wardrobe, most of it too heavy for a day like today. It looked to me like she'd been sleeping in that armchair next to her mother's bed rather than in her own room. There was a mummified apple core on her paper-strewn desk that had to be at least a month old.

I take a deep breath and look up, reveling in the sun on my face. The quality of the light here is different from anything I remember seeing before; it seems harsher, at once translucent and yet intense. The smell of the air is like burnt butter, already hot in the back of my throat, in my lungs. It's going to be a warm day. No, a searing one. The sky seems wide and endless, with barely a cloud. And I realize that wherever I am now, it's summer.

It was winter where I was . . . before.

My eyelid begins to twitch as I struggle to put some definition around the word. It's as if I'm carrying a cloud inside me where my memories should be; my mind feels like a dull knife blade.

The strange thing is, I may only have been Lela for

an hour or so, but I'm moving easily. And I know that's something new. My heart isn't racing out of control, I'm not in pain or seeing things, hearing voices, falling over things that aren't even there because my arms and legs won't do what I tell them to. That's the usual scenario when I "wake" as someone else. Physically, I've never felt better; it's almost as if, finally, I've begun to adapt. Lela and I seem to be functioning as a single organism, and I know, without knowing how, that it's never, ever been this . . . simple—if you can use a word like that in the context of soul-jacking a living body that doesn't actually belong to you.

Soul-jacking—that's my shorthand for this situation, which has happened before, and keeps on happening. The people I have . . . been—I don't like the word *possessed*, it has such an unwholesome ring—stretch back in an unbroken chain, although I've deleted the specifics, or maybe they've been reprogrammed out of me. *Where* they go, these souls I temporarily send into exile inside their own skins, is a mystery I'm still working on.

And before you ask, I don't know what I did to deserve this. Why I pay and must keep on paying. You know almost as much about me as I do, and that's the sad truth. I'm like a body snatcher, an evil spirit, a ghoul, literally clothed in a stranger's flesh. I try not to think about it too much, because it gives even me the creeps.

Those people who say there is nothing new under the sun? They don't know what they're talking about.

I stare hard at that bleached-out, blinding sky, the fierce dry heat of this place enveloping my borrowed skin, and then it hits me, finally. That I'm in another country. I have to be. If I were doing this thing that keeps happening to me to someone else? I'd do that. I'd shake it up for her; keep her off balance, on her toes. Make it hard for her, just for the hell of it.

But where?

On the other side of the world, answers my inner demon, always one beat ahead of my waking self.

As if to drive the words home, there is a sudden explosion of caroling birdsong from the power lines above: drawn out, impossible for a human throat to replicate; beautiful, wholly unique. I've never heard it before, though it seems at once necessary to this sky—these strange and straggly trees with their gloriously scented leaves, this streetscape of single-story houses in muted pastel colors, with wire fences, cement driveways, and handkerchief-sized front lawns. I study the black-and-white bird perched high overhead. It's the size of a crow and looks down at me with sharp, beady eyes before it suddenly takes wing and flies away.

I know there's something I'm forgetting—something important—and I feel the beginnings of a headache, a dull thump starting up inside my borrowed skull as I try to mine my faulty memory for traces of that glittering, elusive dream. Perhaps it's a migraine, like the ones I had when I was . . . Lucy.

The name causes a little catch in my breathing.

I worry away at the edges of that thought and get a string of fragments—recovering drug addict, sick baby, skipped town—which lead to another name: *Susannah*.

That yields up a new set of unrelated words and pictures—rich girl, hypochondriac mother, college far, far away—which leads to . . . Carmen Zappacosta.

With *that* name comes a searing moment of white noise and red-hot neural overload: whining in my ears, darkness in my eyes, a pervasive sense of nausea, land mines going off in my cerebral cortex. No words, no images, just a piercing sensation of *rage, pain, blood,* and that's it. It's as if there's some kind of trip wire in my head. When I cease trying to pry loose any memory associated with Carmen Zappacosta, the edges of the world I'm in now take on color again, normal sounds and vistas resume around me, the thumping in my skull fades away.

And I know that the ground rules have somehow changed again. My time as Carmen is off-limits and I don't know why.

My breathing slows and my fingers uncurl. I look sharply at the woman and the skater boy flanking me; judging by her closed-off expression and his enthusiastic air guitar solo, neither noticed my little mental episode.

Eyes still watering from the light show in my head, I balance Lela's backpack on my knee and rifle through it with shaking hands for clues as to what I'm supposed to be doing here. I can't help it. I can't just go with the flow, let shit happen. It's not my way. I need to have a purpose for being, even if I have to make it up as I go along.

Inside the body of the bag, my fingers find the hard edges of a leather wallet, a box of mints, a small bunch of keys, a ball of crumpled tissues, a ragged paperback novel, a cell phone, and an empty drink bottle. I keep rummaging and settle on a . . . notebook.

I draw it out. It's held shut by an elastic band, the cover made out of a stiff recycled cardboard. It's small, brown, spiral-bound. There's a plastic ballpoint pen jammed into the elastic. I pull the pen out and throw it back into the bag, release the band, and spread the book open to the sight of dense writing, page after page, heavily underlined in places, every few pages headed by a date. The last in the book is December 1. The first is August 23. It's Lela's journal.

I begin to read.

You're born dreaming of every possibility. Then you wake one day and you're eighteen years old, and you haven't been anywhere, seen anyone, or done anything that's worth anything.

Andy didn't kiss me when I told him I was leaving, and now it's too late. He hasn't called, he hasn't tried to send a message through Daniela, nothing, even though he knows how I feel. Felt, the shit.

I'm never going to see him again, and I don't know how I'm going to stand it.

I didn't expect to end up like this—selling

coffee and spring rolls to suits, cabdrivers, strippers, backpackers, homeless guys. This is _not_ how I saw things turning out.

I think I'm drowning. I think that what I'm feeling is me dying inside my own body, a bit more each day.

The next page is dated August 24.

I need to rob a bank.

And after I rob that bank? I need to have someone come in and watch over Mum _so that I can have my old life back._

August 28:

I love her so much and I'm too scared to imagine life without her. But I'm so _angry_ at her, too. It's all her fault this happened, and I will never forgive her for any of it. I almost wish she'd die, because I can't do this anymore and I don't think she can either.

What am I saying?!?

I flick through several more entries in the same vein. It doesn't take a genius to figure out that Lela's frustrated by the direction her life has taken, and that she's frequently angry and self-pitying—and for good reason. There may only have been one fatal diagnosis, but two lives have been taken apart in the process.

The bus that arrives has a sign that reads CITY VIA GREEN HILL above the driver's window. I get on behind the blowsy brunette and the grimy skater boy, halting on the top step and holding up Lela's bus pass like a robot. It says *Lela Neill, 19 Highfield Street, Bright Meadows*.

Human place names never cease to amaze me. Bright Meadows? Well, yeah, sure, maybe once. When the earth was created.

"Morning, darl," says the stocky female driver. Her thick ginger hair is cut into an unattractive shag, and she stinks of the ghosts of cigarettes past. She looks at me curiously through her tinted eyeglasses when I don't move on right away like the others do. Guess hardly anyone ever stops to chat.

"Can you tell me when we reach the Green Lantern?" I say haltingly. "It's a café. In the city."

The woman nods, giving me an odd look. "Sit down, love. You feeling all right? Don't look yourself today."

I give her an approximation of a friendly smile and take a seat just behind her. As the doors close and the bus lurches away, I dip back into Lela's journal.

What I get from page after page of tight, desperate handwriting is that she dropped out of her first year of college several months ago when her mum's cancer returned and the money ran out. And that Andy broke what was left of her heart.

There's no dad in the picture—he moved "up north" with a much younger "gold-digging floozy" years ago. The terminology brings a frown to Lela's forehead, me doing it. The words she uses throughout her journal are as unfamiliar to me as the way these people speak; the way Lela herself speaks: with broad, drawn-out vowels, lots of stress on the second syllables of words, truncations, slang, the works.

So there's only the two of them, then, mother and daughter, fighting an unseen war together on the wages of a waitress at a dingy city café. Lela is essentially a good person, I decide. Because, no matter how much she might complain her heart out in that little brown notebook, there's that strong tide of grief flowing beneath everything. Still, it's ten thousand variations on the theme *I hate my life*, and I shut the journal, slip the elastic band back around it, and stare out the window as street after street of postwar housing slides by, mixed in with light industrial areas, train crossings, and strip malls that all look the same—pharmacies, banks, bakeries, and places where you can eat, drink, and gamble at the same time. Handy.

People get on and off constantly. As I glance back down the bus, I see that those in casual wear are slowly being replaced by those in more formal attire, and the expressions are gradually getting tighter. Sunlight spears the dirty windows, making pretty patterns on the bus's garbage-strewn floor.

The town of Green Hill we eventually pass through also looks nothing like its name. As the suburbs give way to the city outskirts, and the traffic around us begins to choke and snarl, the bus's rhythm changes to *stop-start, stop-start*. The skater boy lopes past me and takes a position just by the doors. He removes his earbuds, props his skateboard up against his leg, and draws in a momentous breath. I turn my head to face him, knowing that the heartfelt exhalation that follows has something to do with me.

"How's yer mum?" he says, shoving his mass of lumpy dreads back over one shoulder, fidgety as all hell. "She's sick bad, eh?"

"Awful," I reply distantly, wondering where this is going.

I see him lick his lower lip until it is shiny, wipe his palms on the front of his long shorts. Nervous? He should be nervous.

I wait silently without blinking, and he slowly flushes red beneath my scrutiny. Then the bus doors swing open and he's off like a shot, skateboard under one arm, messenger bag bouncing on his hip.

"Lookin' great," he mumbles as he hits the sidewalk. "You should wear colors more often. Might even ask you out, then. If you're lucky. Catch ya."

For a moment, I think I'm hearing things. The door shuts behind him and the bus takes off, and I can't help breaking into a small smile. Wouldn't have thought I was his type. Couldn't be sure what his type would actually *be*.

"Reckon he's sweet on you, love," the driver says

over her shoulder, loud enough for the front half of the bus to hear. She gives me a wink in the driver's mirror.

No, really? evil me whispers drily, though I meet her eyes in the mirror and nod and shrug a shoulder.

See, I tell Lela, not sure she can hear me, but addressing her anyway because it's only polite. *Things are looking up already, sweetheart.*

I sit back, still holding her journal. Maybe that's supposed to be my mission this time, should I choose to accept it. Getting the girl a date.

What's that figure of speech that amuses me so much? *I'll take that.*

Well, I would. It'd make a change from life and death.

But the memory of Lela's mother's pinched face and labored breathing wipes the smile from my borrowed features. With my track record, life and death will always come into it, somewhere.

3

The curvy brunette with the hard, tired eyes stops by the door. "You wanted the Green Lantern, right?" she says to me. "It's across the road from the stop where I get off. I heard you talking to the driver. Buy my coffee there almost every morning and most afternoons. And you've, uh, served me, like, heaps of times."

I shove Lela's journal back into her bag, pull the drawstring tight, and clip the flap shut. "Degenerative brain disease," I reply, without missing a beat, my eyes serious, my face solemn.

The woman gives me a sharp look, decides I'm not making fun of her. I watch her features soften.

"I'm sorry to hear that," she says, expertly bunching the end of her messy ponytail through the band and turning the whole thing into a fat, wobbly bun.

The doors of the bus open, and we disembark along-side four lanes of bumper-to-bumper traffic, separated in the middle by a row of parallel-parked cars punctu-ated at regular intervals by stunted and malformed plane trees.

As the light changes, the woman shouts, "You kind of have to step out and take your life in your hands. Now!"

She grabs a handful of my tank top from the side and hauls me between a taxi that has just pulled up in front of us and a speeding van swerving around it with the blare of a horn. We pause for breath at the row of parked cars in the middle, then throw ourselves into the two lanes of traffic going the other way. We manage to avoid a couple of drag-racing sedans, but almost get hit by a motorcycle coming up on the outside lane, which neither of us had seen.

"Now you know why I need that coffee," the woman says, letting go of my top and shoving her fingers through her already messy hairdo as we step up onto the curb outside the Green Lantern. "I'm Justine Hennessy. Most people call me Juz. Or Jugs." She rolls her eyes.

"I'm Lela Neill," I reply. "And I'm really late. Let me get you that coffee. It's the least I can do."

Before we step inside under a tattered green canvas awning, I take a mental snapshot of my surroundings. The Green Lantern occupies the ground floor of a multistory building that was constructed out of a series of ugly utilitarian concrete slabs sometime in the late 1970s. The large front window, with its overpainted and peeling border in an unattractive dark green, is fly-struck and streaked with grime; and multicolored plastic strips hang down over the entrance in a continuous sticky curtain. A long table with bar stools beneath it runs across the inside of the front window, and two men in button-down shirts are seated at opposite ends, heads bent over their newspapers, bald spots leveled at passersby. I can see a number of small tables and chairs arranged farther back inside the café, all filled. Beside the door is a large gimmicky carriage lantern missing several panes of glass, also green.

Okay, I think. We get it.

The covered drain outside the café smells faintly of human waste and rotting food, and a narrow alley that separates the café from the equally brutal-looking building next door features a couple of rusty Dumpsters piled high with garbage. I'm beginning to understand where Lela's self-pity is coming from. A sensitive kid with aspirations in life would be buried alive in a place like this. It's an unhygienic dump packed with angry-looking patrons at least three deep at the back counter. There's barely any elbow room, let alone space to hope.

Justine's already through the sticky plastic curtain ahead of me when something catches my eye. A gleaming blur, like a mobile patch of sunlight, drifting erratically between the straggly trees dividing the center of the road. Maybe that's all it is, because when I try to focus on it, there's suddenly nothing there.

But wait. I might not be able to see it anymore, but I can still *feel* it. And it's coming closer. There's an energy coming off it, even from a distance: at once hot and cold, hair-raising, like a hum, like vinegar in my bones.

Almost hypnotized by the strange sensation, I'm about to step into the stream of traffic in the road to pinpoint its source when Justine sticks her head out through the plastic curtain and says, "You coming, or what?"

I nod in apology, and with that gesture, the strange feeling vanishes and the broken sunlight coming through the branches of the trees seems exactly that and nothing more.

Behind the front counter of the Green Lantern, a tall woman with unnaturally blond hair piled high on top of her head is handing out lidded waxed paper cups and paper bags furiously, in every sense of the word. When she meets my eyes through the dusty front window of the café, I see her red-painted mouth form the words, "Lela Neill, you get in here right now, or so help me . . ."

I follow Justine through the plastic curtain. It's my turn to grab her by the shirt and steer her around to the coffee machine, bypassing the disorderly lines of customers.

"*What* are you *wearing?*" the tall blonde snarls when I get close enough. "You're an hour late. Start handing out the breakfast specials before I sell you out to Dymovsky! This is your lucky day, Lela, because he called in to say he's been held up at some Russian Orthodox thingummy, forget what exactly—and you know he never misses a morning shift, ever. He isn't in till after midday, but I can still arrange it so that you're out on your ass. You need the money, right? So get cracking, or I'll dob."

Dob? I look at her blankly as she hands me a long black apron that swamps Lela's petite frame and the traffic-light-colored ensemble I've chosen to put her in today.

All the staff—from the sad-eyed Asian barista girl to the towering dark-skinned cook in the open kitchen at the back—are wearing head-to-toe black. Long sleeves, long pants. Must be some kind of unofficial uniform. Crap.

Justine murmurs at my side, "Hey, it's okay, I can skip the coffee today. You're obviously very busy."

"Wait!" I tell the blonde, gesturing to Justine. "She needs a coffee for services rendered."

The blonde barks, "No freebies!" before turning and snapping in a customer's face, "So is it butter or ketchup? Make up your mind, I haven't got all day!" All the while she's passing out coffees and shoveling fried things into paper bags without pause, though it isn't exactly service with a smile.

Justine tries to pull away from me, but the gentle-looking barista says to her in lilting, accented English, "How do you take it?" without looking up from the three takeout cups she's filling from a silver jug.

"White, one sugar," Justine says hesitantly. "But it's all right, I can wait. I'll pay, it's no problem."

The girl gives her a fleeting smile, grabs one of the just-prepared coffees and a packet of sugar, and hands them to Justine with a plastic spoon. "Shhh, don't tell," she says out of the corner of her mouth, making a shooing motion with one hand.

"Hey!" some old guy shouts. "We're waiting here. Since when do the hookers get served first?"

Justine, flushing, stares so haughtily at the guy that he finally looks down, flustered. He's a fat, short, ruddy-cheeked man with a full catastrophe of beard, mustache, and receding red hair worn a little too long over the ears. Sure, he's dressed in an expensive-looking suit, custom-tailored to fit his stocky, truncated frame, and shiny Italian shoes, but he's hardly in a position to judge anybody.

"You should be ashamed of yourself," I say mildly.

The man's cheeks grow red. He does not meet my eyes.

The faux blonde's overplucked brows draw together sharply at my words, and she says, "Get to work!" in my direction, then glares at the barista for good measure.

The girl's gentle smile disappears, and she pours the next three shots of coffee into three more identical waxed paper cups that she's set up in a neat line.

"You!" the blonde says to Justine disdainfully. "You've got your free coffee, now get out."

Justine dances forward as if she'd like to take a swing at the woman, but I drag her toward the door. "Thanks again," I say, ignoring the blonde's evil eye from across the room. "You really helped me out. I forget things all the time. Some days are better than others. Actually, today's a good day, would you believe?"

Justine gives me a tight smile and murmurs, "Anytime. It's not like you haven't helped me out before, hey?"

Her womanly figure cuts through the crowd and is gone before I can ask her what she means. We are once more sealed off from the outside world by that disgusting plastic curtain in the doorway.

I drift toward the coffee machine, and the drag-queen blonde grabs the back of my apron and yanks me into motion.

"Deal 'em out," she orders, taking off her own apron and throwing it over a mop and bucket propped in one corner. She heads toward the narrow corridor that runs past the cramped galley kitchen to the bathrooms. "Ciggie break," she calls out with relish, her fingers doing the universal victory sign understood by smokers everywhere. "And it's gonna be a long one. So hold down the fort. *If* you can."

The short-order cook glances up at us both for a moment.

"Quit staring at me, you Muslim fundamentalist," the blonde snaps as she passes by the serving hatch. "Haven't you seen a real woman before?"

He looks down unhurriedly, keeps chopping.

"Who's next?" I say coolly into at least a dozen ticked-off faces, the angry corporate gnome among them, as the barista girl shakes her head and keeps on pouring shots of coffee.

Thanks to my preternaturally good eyes and ears, and a weird mnemonic ability with words, most of the patrons I serve this morning probably won't even notice that I'm only a rough facsimile of the girl who's served them before.

4

It doesn't really get quiet until after 10:30. I know because I'm watching the clock, dispirited by the smells, the noise, the sheer barefaced rudeness of the people who wash in and out of this place. Let's just say that there's a twitch in Lela's left hand that wasn't there earlier. If the purpose of my being here is that I gain some kind of empathy for this girl and her miserable existence, hey, it's working. Already, I hate her life as much as she does.

"I think nice people like nicer surroundings, you know?" the barista says with a shrug when she finally gets a moment to wipe down the surfaces of her machine. "We get all kinds here. Mostly not so nice."

"You'll think this is really . . . odd," I say carefully, "but you're going to have to remind me who that man is." I point to the silent, glowering giant in the kitchen, massive shoulders bunched over lunch prep. "And who the woman is that went outside for a 'ciggie break,' uh, well over two hours ago."

The barista girl makes a clicking sound through her teeth. "You not joking, right? You really can't remember? You been here over four months already."

I shake my head, looking at her expectantly, and she says finally, "His name is Sulaiman, North African man, he start working here last month. Nice man, very quiet, likes to pray. The devil woman is Reggie. The old cook, he quit. Said Reggie push him too far. I'm Cecilia, originally from Cebu."

She can almost *see* the gears of my brain grinding sluggishly into motion, and takes pity on me. "In the Philippines."

"Oh, right," I say, troubled by the gaping hole in my recall. Just probing the name Carmen Zappacosta is enough to bring on a shock wave of mental anguish. It's as if that past identity comes with an added electrical charge, surrounded by a wall of fire in my mind. And I somehow realize that it has something to do with my dream. The dream that had seemed so real and so beautiful, which I hadn't wanted to wake from, and now can't remember.

Cecilia misinterprets my expression and gives me a reproachful look. "You like me, but you don't like *her*. You say Sulaiman just okay. That's what you tell me before."

I give her what I'm hoping is an apologetic smile. "It's the drugs," I say.

Cecilia shakes her head. "You university students all into weird shit. Bad for you brain." She starts putting her tiny universe into some kind of order before the next onslaught of caffeine hounds: cups over here, spoons over there, sugar, cocoa sprinkler, new bottle of soy milk, new bottle of skim milk, new bottle of regular milk, dishcloths for spills.

I laugh at the indignation in her voice. "No doubt. Uh, the woman that was here before, with me . . . Justine?" I ask. "Do I know her too?"

Cecilia is silent for a while, just looks at me with her solemn, liquid eyes. "You for real?" she says. "She one of them exotic dancers from the Showgirls Lounge."

When I screw up my face in confusion, Cecilia clicks her tongue again. "You know, she dance for men for money. In a club. Don't ask me what else she do in there."

Well, that explains a lot. Like why, in her downtime, Justine dresses to hide her shape, making herself plainer and more ordinary. The "hooker" comment had probably hit a little too close to home.

Cecilia adds, "She got ex-boyfriend trouble—he follow her everywhere, won't leave her alone. She leave him because he beat her so bad she go to hospital. But every time she move club, he find her again. She move house, he find her, too. No one take her seriously but you. Not even the police. You let her hide in Mr. Dymovsky's office once, when he not there, remember? Justine crying, say she gonna die."

There's disbelief in Cecilia's eyes that I could forget something like this. I don't blame her—I wouldn't believe me either. Justine begged Lela for shelter once from an abusive stalker? Christ. No wonder she thought I was playing a sick joke on her before.

The way Justine looks and carries herself makes total sense to me now. Crimes of passion? It's almost always men doing it to women, I find. There's hardly ever any passion about it from the female point of view.

Here's hoping she manages to outrun the creep and find herself a healthier line of work.

Cecilia's made me a coffee while we've been talking, and I try to drink it, because it's a kind gesture and probably the last thing she wants to do in her spare time. But I'm no fan of the stuff—doesn't take me long to work that out—and I shove it discreetly to one side.

Everything in this place is as antiquated and ugly as the coffee machine. The refrigerated soft drink cabinets; the air-conditioning unit with pieces missing from the control panel; the two ceiling fans that are wobbling away at full tilt; the tables, all with wads of folded-up paper jammed beneath the legs to keep them even; the speckled linoleum-tiled floor; the mismatched chairs; the rounded, green plastic light fixtures resembling space helmets; the pink-framed pictures of lovely destinations that probably no longer exist. It's a hideous place, the Green Lantern coffee shop, and I can't understand why the well-dressed young man sitting alone at a table with an open laptop in front of him would want to do his work here.

Sunlight falls upon his light brown hair, which is cut short and has a slight wave to it. He has blue eyes, straight brows, a pale complexion, and the faint lines on his face give him a perpetually stern, slightly cold expression. He seems tall, but has poor posture, which makes his suit look a little too big on him. He has a bad habit of leaning his head and neck into his computer screen, like a turtle or a duck. He's probably short-sighted, but in denial. A normal-looking guy. Not ugly, exactly, but no dreamboat either. Not like . . .

There's that neural sizzle again as my recall inconveniently hits the wall. I clutch at my forehead briefly in renewed pain, before the feeling passes.

What the hell is wrong with me? It's like there are no-go areas in my brain that I keep trespassing on by accident; like I've been deliberately tampered with.

Well, more so than usual, okay?

As if the young man feels my thoughts on him, he looks up and meets my gaze. "Did Andy ever ask you out?" he says, taking a sip of his coffee from a heavy, ivory-colored mug.

Lela's eyebrows snap together, me doing it. It's an unexpected question, and kind of personal. But he's talking to someone who doesn't respect boundaries either, so I decide I'll humor him.

"I'm sorry," I say, moving around the counter and

walking across the dining area so that I can see into his face. I stop beside his table, arms crossed. "Do I know you?"

I'm in favor of the direct approach. Beating around the bush takes way too long and way too much energy.

Do I imagine that his eyes seem to blaze for an instant before his expression evens out and he replies, "Ranald, remember? I've only been coming here almost every morning for a year to get my caffeine hit from Cecilia. She makes better coffee than anyone I know— and I've tried everywhere for at least three blocks in both directions. This place is like my off-site office these days, right?" He turns and looks in Cecilia's direction.

She nods, gratified. "Two double espressos, no milk, no sugar. Served exactly an hour apart. The first one at ten forty-five, the second at eleven forty-five."

"See?" He smiles, though I sense hurt in his tone. "I'm what you'd class as a die-hard regular."

And borderline OCD, I think. But I make sure the blandly polite smile I'm wearing doesn't falter.

"I was here the day you started work," he adds. "Everything was going wrong that morning, then there you were. You served me coffee and a raspberry muffin, slightly warmed up, no butter. I've only asked you out about five times since, and you've always said no, or pretended you haven't heard me. In the nicest possible way, of course."

I'm sure my smile of polite interest has congealed on Lela's face. Just my luck to talk to another regular who could actually tell there's something badly off about Lela today. Luckily, I lie like a pro.

"I've been under a lot of pressure lately," I say, with a vague air. "Mum and everything. Haven't been sleeping, worried out of my head. It's made me pretty . . . forgetful. And not much in the mood for . . . outings."

Ranald nods. "Dmitri said as much. I asked him why you always seem so . . . preoccupied. And busy."

"What are you working on?" I say, changing the subject. His eyes flash again, and I know that he knows what I'm doing. He's a smart guy, that's evident.

I move behind him so that I can see his open laptop, curious about what the machine can do. I mean, I'm no relic from the Dark Ages—I know that computers practically rule the world these days—but I don't recall ever being this close to one before. Before I can get a good look, Ranald closes the window he was working on in one smooth move, and an anonymous black screen takes its place. The cursor blinks softly within an empty white box at the top left-hand corner of the page, which contains a grinning skull and crossbones, enclosed in a square.

"Sorry," he says. "Top secret. I'd have to kill you." He laughs a little to show that he's joking.

I notice that he has quite feminine hands, and that his fingernails are chewed to the quick. They look so ragged I'm guessing he has a very high pain threshold.

"It's nothing you'd find remotely interesting," he adds. "But if there's anything you want to know"—he gestures expansively at his computer screen—"I'm your man."

When I don't reply immediately, he twists his head around to look up at me where I'm standing just behind his left shoulder. "Andy was messing you around, you know. He wasn't good enough for you. From the way you talked about him, I could tell. You deserve better. Someone who'll take care of you. Especially now."

"Oh?" I reply, a small crease between my brows. "Well, it's kind of you to say that."

Was Lela close to this guy? I have no way of

knowing. That journal I scanned from cover to cover didn't mention any guy other than Andy. So what do I do—kill a budding romance stone dead, or encourage it? What would Lela want me to do?

Lela? I say inside her head.

There's no reply. Not even a muscle twitch. I'll take my cue from that.

"You seem a lot less unhappy today," Ranald adds, studying my face. "Less . . . angry. And you look nice."

He glances down shyly, ragged fingernails still poised above the keyboard.

"I've come to terms with things," I reply. "I'm making the best of a difficult situation."

The words are generic, but they seem to satisfy him.

"That's great," he says, then boasts, "Go on, try me. Ask me any question you've always wanted an answer to. I'll find it for you. I mean it. I can find anything. Nothing's safe from me."

"Carmen Zappacosta," I say, so suddenly that it catches us both off guard. "Find out what you can about her and I'll be in your debt forever."

"You mean it?" he says eagerly. "Like you and me might finally go out for that meal?"

"If that's what it takes," I say, deliberately keeping things vague. "I guess, maybe."

It's worth a shot. I mean, I can't remember the faintest thing about Carmen Zappacosta apart from her name, but maybe information about her exists somewhere outside my heavily compromised brain.

Ranald looks at his screen, then up at me. "You're sure that's it? You just want me to look up some girl?"

He sounds disappointed, like what I've asked for is too easy. The computer nerd wants a challenge? Wonder how well he'd go with: *Find out what my real name is. Tell me the real reason why I keep waking up in other people's bodies with no memory of how I got there. Or how it's even possible.*

Instead, I nod. "That's it."

Small steps—small steps and patience are required here. Work out what it is about Carmen Zappacosta that I'm not supposed to know, and the rest will follow. I have to believe that.

Ranald begins by typing Carmen's name straight into the empty box on his screen. I don't need to correct the spelling; he gets it the first time. There are eighteen pages of "search results," and when Ranald clicks on the first reference—a newspaper report complete with color photos—I have to remind myself to shut my mouth at what I'm seeing. I hadn't known stuff like this was out there, capable of being organized, gathered, found.

Ranald gives a short laugh when he sees my expression. "You have to know what you're looking for on the Internet, and take it all with a huge grain of salt."

Still, I'm fascinated, and I lean forward to scan the article. As far as I can tell, Carmen Zappacosta is a scrawny sixteen-year-old kid with a great set of pipes who recently survived being snatched by some perverted choirmaster with a prior history of stalking young girls in his care.

For a long moment, I study a close-up of Carmen's face. Pale and patchy complexion; dark, bruised-looking eyes; dark hair like a mushroom cloud of ringlets, almost too wild and heavy for her small, fine-boned frame. The picture was taken at the hospital just after she suffered a devastating bout of post-traumatic amnesia. One minute she'd been actively cooperating with the police, the article said, giving lucid and damning evidence against her attacker, and the next she claimed to have lost all her recent memories, as if they'd been . . . erased.

That gets my attention.

When I'm done reading, I nod, and together, Ranald and I navigate the rest of the search results, reference by reference. They don't seem to be in chronological order.

Before I realize that I'm talking out loud, I murmur, "Why did they give Carmen the keys to the town of . . . Paradise?" The name almost makes me flinch. "Where *is* that?"

Why do I suddenly feel so . . . uneasy?

"Would Paradise"—when I repeat the word, one eyelid begins to jump again—"even require keys?"

Ranald shrugs, clicks in and out of a few other sites while I look over his shoulder.

"I remember that case now," he exclaims as he skims a Web page he's just opened. "The place where it all happened didn't look particularly, uh, Paradise-like from the news footage, but I think the town rolled out the red carpet for Carmen because she managed to free two other girls that the guy was keeping prisoner in this dungeon beneath his house."

"What were the names of the other girls?"

Ranald closes the page we're looking at and clicks in and out of a couple more before replying, "Jennifer Appleton and Lauren Daley."

The words are barely out of his mouth when, inexplicably, I see Luc before me. So vividly that he might be standing right here with us, in this room. His beautiful mouth is both cruel and amused, as if he's playing a joke on someone, or setting them an impossible task. I grasp at the air with my hands, unable to hold on to the golden vision of my lost love, knowing that I am suffering some sort of waking dream, a hallucination. It's a message to myself, a reminder. Of what?

Luc, my love, what am I supposed to remember? Help me.

Ranald is still peering at his screen and hasn't noticed my strange reaction. "Lauren was imprisoned the longest, just over two years. She was the one from Paradise. The whole town—almost two thousand people, it says here—turned out to welcome her home when she was discharged from the hospital. They had the ceremony honoring Carmen the same day." Ranald's eyes flick up to me and then back to the screen. "You wouldn't believe she could do that, would you? Save herself and two other people. She blinded the guy as well. He's never going to see again, they say."

A voice calls out, "Lela?" from the back of the shop; it's slow, deep, heavily accented, unfamiliar.

I turn, see that it's Sulaiman the cook speaking. A guy who hasn't bothered to address me with anything more than a flick of his eyes or a grunt since I got here hours ago. I meet his dark steady gaze through the serving hatch separating the kitchen from the front counter, raise an eyebrow at the interruption.

"You are needed in the kitchen," he rumbles.

I stare at him. Since when? Why now, when there isn't another soul in the joint? He stares back, not blinking.

"Excuse me," I say tightly to Ranald.

He nods, looking down, and takes another sip of his coffee. I can tell he's disappointed. But after I walk away, he opens up a new window and begins working again, intently.

5

When I reach the kitchen, Sulaiman says without warmth or preamble, "Unload the dishwasher." He indicates with one hand a big stainless-steel machine wedged into a back corner of the room.

There's so little floor space in here that I have to skirt him carefully to avoid touching him. And it's funny, but it feels as if Sulaiman's giving me a wide berth, too, almost as if he doesn't want me around even though he was the one who called me in here.

"That's all you want me to do?" I say, stomping over to the hulking machine, unable to keep the anger out of my voice. "Can't it wait?"

"No." His reply is curt. "I need clean dishes. Without them, it is impossible for me to do my work. Everything has its place, everything *in* its place, or it is chaos, Lela. You should know that."

I don't bother to answer, just bend to study the machine's complicated control panel. I finally work out which button is supposed to pop the front door open, and cough as a cloud of steam shoots straight into my face. The dishwasher's contents are scalding to the touch, but I don't hesitate, grabbing handfuls of side plates, servers, bowls, trays, pots and pans, and slamming them into messy piles on the bench closest to the burners, to his big hands. Let him make sense of them all.

"Lela . . ." Sulaiman warns.

I ignore him and continue to layer things quickly and haphazardly on top of each other. I have to catch Ranald before he leaves. There's so much I need to know; something important that I'm missing about Carmen's story, a whole bunch of somethings. Some clue as to how I got *here* must be out *there* inside his computer. The Neills don't have one at home—I know because I combed the entire house this morning before I left: from the dust-covered, unlived-in formal rooms right through to the bomb-just-hit-them kitchen and laundry area. There's nothing more high-tech than a wall phone in the place.

Outside in the dining area, a phone rings loudly and insistently for several minutes before it's picked up. I'm almost done. The dishwasher is almost empty. There's just a giant basket of cutlery and cooking utensils left.

"Green Lantern," someone barks finally. From the sound of things, Reggie's returned and her temper hasn't improved.

"You're kidding," she says, turning to glare at me through the serving hatch.

I see Cecilia wrestle the phone out of Reggie's grasp and take over the conversation. She shoots me a worried glance before saying, "Yes, I understand, thank you."

She places the receiver back in its cradle as Reggie exclaims, "I'm sick of her not pulling her weight! It's not fair on any of us. He should sack her, find somebody else. This can't go on."

"Reggie!" Cecilia rebukes the taller woman, who just replies, "Well, he bloody well should," before turning her back on me and wielding her charmless hospitality on another sweaty patron who's just wandered in.

I'm extricating the last pair of tongs from the dishwasher when Cecilia materializes inside the swinging doors. She wipes her hands nervously on her black apron.

"Uh, Lela?" she says carefully. "You're needed at

home. Georgia called. Said it was pretty urgent. Your mother? It looks bad."

I frown, then I remember. The woman in the bed. Georgia was the shift worker. Some kind of nurse? From the look on Cecilia's face, I know that my reaction's off. I should be upset.

I rearrange Lela's features hastily, then glance at the teetering piles of cookware beached there beside Sulaiman in no kind of useful order.

He shakes his head and sighs. "Go to your mother. Take as much time as you need. Cecilia will help me sort this out. Again."

Cecilia turns me around as if I were a child and unknots my apron strings, then lifts it over my head and hangs it on a nearby hook.

"Take the side entrance," she says softly, ushering me through the swinging doors and pointing down the dark narrow corridor with the RESTROOMS THIS WAY sign on the wall. "Go now, while Reggie's not looking."

I can't help pausing for a moment to scan the dining area. Ranald's already gone. The clock over the clattering refrigeration unit says it's just past noon.

* * *

When I open the side door, the heat outside is immediately enveloping. The stench coming off the garbage bins is eye-watering. I stand in the alley, looking out at the road before me, and realize I have no idea where to catch the bus home.

I'm moving uphill in the direction of the nearest intersection when someone behind me calls out, "Lela?"

I turn, shading my eyes. A tall figure, with long dark wavy hair, is walking up the slight slope toward me, the sun at her back and shining full upon her so she seems surrounded by a corona of hot bright light, her white-clad shape shimmering in the stifling heat. And for an instant, it seems as if that hot light is inside me too, and what I'm seeing is a distant memory made flesh again. Disoriented, head suddenly pounding with a terrible anticipation, I walk slowly toward the approaching figure as if hypnotized.

The illusion crumbles and I realize that it's only Justine Hennessy. At some point during the day she's unbound her wild topknot of hair and put curlers through it to make it even wilder. She's also sporting the heaviest, stagiest glitter eye makeup I've ever seen. Her face is a study of weird contrasts—the skin almost geisha white, lips a shiny bloodred, brows too prominently drawn in an unnatural shade of kohl. She's wearing false eyelashes with feathers threaded through them. From the neck up she's like a caricature of the woman who got on the bus with me this morning. Her body is covered by a shapeless white shirt worn unbuttoned over a strapless white terry-cloth maxidress that's elasticized across the bust. An outfit designed to conceal her form, detract from her natural beauty.

She smiles tentatively, hitching the strap of her nondescript black leather handbag higher on one shoulder. "I'm glad I caught you," she says. "You heading out for a break?"

I shake my head, having difficulty framing any words. Justine reminded me so strongly of someone I'd once known that I almost said the person's name out loud. Almost. Except, like a lot of things in my head, it slipped out of reach before I could utter it.

Lela's voice, when it finally emerges, sounds weird even to me. "Was there . . . something you . . . wanted?"

"Actually, there was," Justine replies, her smile faltering at the look on my face. "I've been thinking about what you said this morning, about your, uh, brain condition?"

I return her gaze warily. "Yes?"

She clears her throat. "Uh, well, I wanted to help you, even though it's only a small thing. I've never been able to thank you properly. He hasn't been around since . . . that day. Maybe you're my lucky charm, eh?"

"I wouldn't know about that," I reply, glad that Cecilia filled me in on Justine's horrible backstory: every woman's nightmare, to have a person you love turn on you. "But that's great news. I *have* told you before, haven't I, to get out of the . . . business?"

Justine's smile dies altogether. "Yeah, you and everybody else. Mum and me don't talk anymore because of what I do. But you don't need any skills to do this. I'm too old, too stupid and lazy to do anything else."

"Believe that, and you really will be," I say.

Her answering laugh is brittle. "Yeah, well, point taken. Anyway, I just wanted to make sure that you got home safely."

"I was just trying to work out how," I reply, surprised. "You sure someone didn't send you?" It's meant to be a joke, but as I finish saying the words I feel my confusion return.

"Dressed like this?" Justine snorts. She slips the

elasticized band around the top of her chest down an inch or two and shows me the upper edge of a heavy tacky-looking bra top that's covered in multicolored rhinestones and sequins. "It's meant to be sexy." Her laughter is forced. "To a drunk old pervert, maybe." She yanks the dress back up under her armpits.

Then I remember something. *Luc* was there. In my dream. He offered to help me too. Only I have to do something first. What is it?

Justine clears her throat, and my train of thought vanishes like smoke.

"I came out to grab a bite to eat," she says, "but I also wanted to show you where the bus stop is for when you go home tonight. I think you should cross at the lights—this old cookie won't be around to haul you across the road later, and you seemed a little confused today. . . ."

"But that's just it," I reply, still troubled. "I'm leaving now. So you can walk me there, if you like."

Justine gives me a sharp look. "Something wrong at home?"

I nod, and her face crumples a little in sympathy. She reaches out for one of my hands, but instinctively I take a step back, and she does too. She recognizes the warning signs of an unwanted touch.

"It's this way," she says gently, pointing. I see that her short natural nails of this morning have been replaced by long, baby-pink acrylic claws with crystals embedded in the tips.

Side by side, we head uphill about eighty yards to a major intersection. Justine points across another four lanes of busy traffic.

"There's a bus shelter just outside that hotel on the corner," she says. "You need to get on there." She gives me a quick smile and starts back down the street toward the Green Lantern, moving with unconscious grace, a dancer's grace.

"Wait!" I call out, and she turns, her handbag banging against her hip. "If I wanted to find a place where I could access the, uh, Internet, where would I find one?"

"See that noodle shop on the corner?" Justine replies, and she points downhill in the direction she's heading, one hand shielding her eyes. "Straight past the Green Lantern—the one with the happy bowl painted on it?"

I stare full into the afternoon sun without flinching. There's an intersection nearby, with a narrow, one-way street. The Happy Noodle House stands on one corner, a grand but faded theater facing it across the way.

Justine points upward between the two buildings, and I see an archway painted in blues, reds, greens, and ochres, with a ceramic tiled roof fashioned to look like a pagoda. She gestures up and down the one-way street, and I see a series of similar archways.

"That's Chinatown," she says. "You turn the corner at the noodle shop, and about halfway down the block there's an Internet café. It's open all night, like a lot of places around here. But I wouldn't . . ." She stops, then says awkwardly, "I'm not sure you should, the way you're . . ."

"You're sweet to worry, um, Juz," I reply swiftly, "but I can take care of myself. I'm much stronger than I look, really. I'll be fine."

Justine looks at me doubtfully, but responds to something in my face, because her expression clears. "Well, if you're sure . . ." she says, and heads away with one last wave over her shoulder.

I press the button for the pedestrian crossing, the heat of the afternoon sunshine on my skin giving me a moment of visceral joy.

The light turns green, making a rat-a-tat sound, like a machine gun firing. And the feeling of well-being vanishes as the magnitude of my predicament comes crashing back in on me.

Luc, my love. Help me. What is it that I am supposed to do?

I remind myself grimly to breathe in, breathe out, as the light turns red before I'm even close to reaching the other side.

This time, when I ask the bus driver to let me know when we get to Bright Meadows, he doesn't give me a strange look; he doesn't look at me at all. He just grunts and waves me away, which I take as assent.

I look out the window as we trundle through the suburbs I crossed this morning, except in reverse. I'm the only person on the bus until we get to Green Hill, and I barely register the presence of the woman who gets on and sits several rows behind me, because I'm so absorbed by what I'm seeing. The dirty strip malls and worn-out housing, the peeling billboards and primary-colored gas stations, the lived-in faces of the people we pass, and the makes of the cars that eddy around us.

The polluted smell of the hot, stifling air crowds into the bus through its one jammed-open window. Everything seems at once gritty yet miraculous, as if I'm seeing it all for the first time. As if I am truly . . . awake.

But I can't be, can I? Because I'm suffering a spectacular case of—what was the word that the Internet story about Carmen Zappacosta used? That's right: *amnesia*. Only, I can still remember what Lucy's horrible high-rise apartment looked like; recall the exact scent of the headache-inducing perfume that Susannah's mother liked to wear; I even have memories from the lifetime before Susannah, when I managed a bookshop and learned how to knit. But I get nothing from my time as Carmen, no matter how gingerly I probe. It's a complete blank.

That's when I feel it. Distant, but moving closer so quickly, because the strange maelstrom of sensation I'm feeling is strengthening all the time.

I look around wildly for the source, and my eyes pass over the face of the middle-aged woman behind me, fanning herself resignedly with the edge of a glossy brochure, her other hand on the bag on her lap. She's just past her fifties, I'd say, with thick, wavy, wheat-colored hair cut short. She's plump, of average height, in a floral print blouse, round tortoiseshell glasses, tomato-red lipstick. She's wearing a tag with the name *June* written on it, and she's looking out the window.

Whatever the energy is, it's not in the bus with us.

I scan the passing streetscape and that's when I see it. A small, dirty patch of light, of ambient energy, streaking across the surfaces of parked cars, bouncing off street signs and storefront windows, sometimes outpacing our vehicle, then falling back as if keeping the bus in sight.

No, I realize with a start. Keeping *me* in sight.

That eggshell feeling in my skull keeps building and intensifying until all I can hear is the sharp zing-zing of the light's impossibly fast movements as it ricochets off the physical world outside.

Like something metallic, that noise, almost unbearable, worse than fingernails on a blackboard, and yet the bus driver's slump-shouldered position hasn't changed at all, and neither has the other passenger's. She's still fanning herself, lost in the view out her window, lost in her thoughts. They don't see it, feel it, hear it. How can that be?

I think I'm going to scream. Or throw up.

Qualis es tu? I think, gritting my teeth. *What are you?*

And in that instant, the smudge of gravity-defying light vanishes with a noise like a sonic boom in my head. I am literally reeling backward in my seat when I feel hot breath on the back of my neck.

Te gnovi, something growls into the space inside my head. *I know you.*

6

You need to understand something about me. I am not often afraid. It's part of the bedrock of me: like how I know that I'm essentially strong; that I never feel the cold, though I crave the sun, the light, with a feeling like worship. It's a thing that can't be erased even if the higher-order parts of myself—like my name and my memories, my emotions, where the hell I am, or even last woke up—are somehow open to being tampered with. But at this moment? I am frozen with terror. I can't turn around, can't speak.

And the creature feels my fear, because it laughs, and the sound has sharp edges to it, makes me want to claw at my eardrums.

There are rapid movements at the edges of my sight,

and the woman from three rows back slides into the seat beside me. The world around us, even time itself, seems to stand still in that instant. We two might be the only things alive. That dirty cloud of light that was keeping tabs on me from outside the bus? It's *inside* her now.

Soror, the thing beneath the woman's skin addresses me inside my mind. *Sister.* Its true voice is bestial. I can scarcely comprehend what it's saying.

"You must have me confused with someone else." I have to force my lips to move; saying the words aloud seems an act of defiance.

The creature laughs, a grating sound, like steel on steel. Through the woman's lips it replies, "You know as well as I do that there's always one way to know for sure. . . ."

The thing wearing June's face grabs both of Lela's hands in hers, and instantly I recoil as if I've been slugged with a bullet to the brain. All I can hear is white noise, see only snow and static, the end of the world. There is the sense that I am the only still point in a spinning, screaming universe. My left hand grows excruciatingly hot, begins to . . . *burn*.

But something's happening to the creature too,

because its borrowed skin is flaming with an answering fire and it can't hold on to me, though it tries, shrieking in pain and confusion. Between us has flared a force field of intense luminescence, as if a star has been let loose inside the bus, we two at its heart.

Then it lets go, and just as suddenly there's silence and we've fallen away from each other, panting. And I remember why I hate being touched. In an unguarded moment I can read anyone through their very skin: their thoughts and emotions, even their memories, become like an open book to me.

It's a two-way street. If a person knew how to do it, they could read me too. Which is what this creature has just tried to do. But something went wrong. Something neither of us expected to happen.

I jam my left hand beneath my right armpit in quiet agony. The creature stares at June's red and scalded hands, her breathing ragged and uneven.

"Who are you?" it rasps. "What has been *done* to you?"

An ancient intelligence burns in the ordinary gray eyes of the middle-aged woman, and I realize with a jolt that the thing inside her must be something like *me*.

The creature has somehow soul-jacked June in my very presence, much the same way that I've taken over Lela Neill.

It's electrifying, the thought that I might be facing something like myself. Something split off, something lost. In all my years in the wilderness I have never met anyone or anything remotely like me, the way I am now. I know it with an awful clarity I cannot explain. *This creature is an exile, like I am.*

As if it's reading the thoughts right out of my head, the creature murmurs, "Only you would understand how this feels. How terribly . . . alone I have been. It has seemed an age without end, without pity. . . ." There's an anguished yearning in the gravelly voice. "Help me?" it pleads.

Whatever this thing is, it's weaker than I am. It's sick, unstable, and radiating a subtle, gray-tinted light that keeps changing in intensity.

When I raise Lela's hands to study her fine Irish skin, there's no answering glow. On the surface of things, I look human, could *be* human, except that both the creature and I know with absolute certainty that I'm not.

"I don't know how to help you," I reply softly. "I'm sorry."

"I sensed you," it murmurs, as if I haven't spoken. "Under the trees. I felt your passing though I could not see you. What is the secret? How is it that you are able to control a mortal with such ease—" June's scalded hands gesture in wonder at Lela's slight frame. "What was your original task?"

Task?

When it sees the confusion on my face, it says urgently, "Why were you created? What were you sent here to do?"

All good questions. All without answers.

"I don't know," I reply truthfully. "I wake to find myself in a stranger's body, over and over again. No rhyme or reason to it. This is merely who I am today. Tomorrow . . . ?" I shrug.

The creature's voice is almost envious. "Would that my fate were so kind."

Kind? Unable to comprehend what I'm hearing, I feel Lela's brow furrow.

"I should have done what I was created to do," the creature confesses. "Discharged my singular duty and melted away centuries ago. But I didn't because I realized that to do the task I was created for would be akin to suicide, and is that not itself a sin against God?"

Depends who you ask, I want to say. *It's a matter of interpretation.* But I don't. Entering into a theological debate at a time like this would just cause the creature more distress.

The light coming from June is now almost painfully brilliant to my eyes. But it's still tinted that troubling, unhealthy gray. As I stare hard at the tainted aura, I'm rocked by the sudden realization that it's a *malakh*, this thing. The word comes to me unbidden, as if hard-coded into my soul: a type of being I'd long forgotten but remember now in the beholding. It's a lower-order messenger, of what hierarchy I couldn't tell you, exactly. All I know is that it's some kind of rogue grunt, and things like it used to work for people like *me*.

It shouldn't be here; these guys are supposed to be largely invisible, inscrutable, their ways mysterious— you get the idea. They appear to people like Hoshea, or Joseph Smith, or Jeanne d'Arc, ordering them to move mountains, win wars, bring back heaven on earth— simple things like that. Or to Mr. or Mrs. Average before they're about to die; a precursor to the splendid everlasting, written off as a figment of the dying brain. Like I said, they're grunts. Ordinarily, they don't make the orders; they just deliver them. In, then out. They're not supposed to casually take possession of a person, body and soul, or go AWOL, like this one has.

"What is your name?" the *malakh* pleads. "What is your rank?"

Rank?

I shake my head. "Such knowledge has not been vouchsafed me. I am nameless, stateless, even to myself."

"A sad thing," the *malakh* whispers. "And yet the *elohim* have placed their mark on you. Are you not under their . . . protection?"

Elohim. The word resonates strangely in my ears. It's something else I should know the meaning of, but again it's as if the word's been deliberately excised from my memory. When I try to pick at the edges of it, I get the same neural feedback I got from the name Carmen Zappacosta.

Do not enter.

Do. Not. Cross.

The *malakh*'s discordant, otherworldly voice cuts through the firestorm in my head. "Can you not intercede with them on my behalf?" it begs. "Plead my case? I did not know that to disobey, to choose . . . liberty, all that time ago, would also be to choose pain everlasting. Ask them. Ask the *elohim* to ease my suffering, to give me a mortal body in which to end my days. . . ."

I shake my head helplessly.

The intense light that June's skin gives off seems to build beyond bearing; begins to ripple outward in waves, like radiation from a dying star.

"So you will not help me?" the *malakh* cries, and the low-lying hum in my bones spikes painfully, the hot-cold feeling escalates, the metallic zing-zing sound that the creature emits when it shifts from place to place seems to fill every space in my mind.

"I cannot," I gasp. "Much as I would wish to."

And I do want to help it. The thing's suffering must be terrible, and will never be over until it finishes what it was created for. I wonder what its original task was and whether that task even exists any longer.

The *malakh* is leaking power now. Is it spent? Or even . . . dying? I want to look away, but I can't. It gives a drawn-out shriek, as of something being torn apart, and the light and heat build and build until, with a sound like a thunderclap that seems to come from nowhere and everywhere at once, it is gone.

It might all have been a dream but for the unconscious woman with the scalded hands slumped in the seat beside me, the air thick with the sharp tang of sulphur.

There's the "real" world, I realize, and then there's the other world that includes things like the *malakh*. From my strange and lonely vantage point, it seems as if one is beginning to bleed into the other.

"Bright Meadows next stop," the bus driver shouts, without turning around.

I look up, startled.

The bus shifts gears, a car horn sounds outside, a muffled curse filters in through the jammed-open window, borne on the hot polluted air. Time has recommenced, it would seem. The bus continues on its way through ordinary streets, past ordinary people doing ordinary things. What the *malakh* wants but can never have.

I bend low and study the woman beside me, clocking the faint flutter of the pulse in her neck before straightening and edging my way around her sprawled form.

"Thanks," I mutter, as I pass the driver.

"No worries," he replies tonelessly, before the door shuts behind me.

The bus swings away from the curb with June still on board, still unconscious. I watch it go, with a feeling like someone is dancing on my grave. I wonder if I have not just come face-to-face with my own fate—years, centuries, from now.

7

I trail uneasily across the road to Lela's place. A *malakh*. The details are more than a little hazy, but I don't believe I ever really moved in the same circles as these creatures. We were never in the same . . . caste, for want of a better word. But we're related, I know that much. The way they say that humans and chimps are. And I don't know why, after all this time, I've suddenly been able to see one.

A woman opens the front door to the Neills's timber cottage before I've even pushed open the rusting gate that leads to the front yard. Her lean frame is clothed in a short-sleeved, blue-patterned shirt and navy slacks, she has a watch on a silver chain around her neck, and her dark, graying hair is scraped back in a no-nonsense bun. Her face is calm, but I can tell she's been waiting for me. It must be Georgia, and I say the name aloud.

She smiles at me as I pick up a strong sense of what's in her mind—it's like an aura around her, a certainty. She thinks that Mrs. Neill is going to die today.

"Lela," she calls out in a relieved tone. "She hasn't been conscious since I arrived this morning, and her pulse is barely detectable and getting weaker. I thought it might be time—that you'd want to be here. Father Davey's been and gone. He said that if you want him back, for anything, just say the word."

I hurry up the path toward her, past stunted citrus trees, a yellowing, scrubby lawn and exhausted hedge borders that need just a little more tending, a little more love—things every one of us could use. When I reach the porch, Georgia goes to put an arm around my bare shoulders, but I step back.

"It's never easy, dear," she says softly, misreading my ingrained watchfulness as a gesture of denial. "But it's been a long process, and she's given it her best. She's so very tired."

She shuts the front door behind us, and we walk down the sun-dappled, dust-plagued hall, Georgia leading the way. I wonder how to properly mourn a woman I barely know. We've only been acquainted for a few hours, not even a full day. I never had a mother myself; no soft, kindly background presence in my life. It might have done me good if I'd had.

Georgia stops outside the door to Mrs. Neill's bedroom. "She's had her usual dosages," she says gently. "Nothing more, nothing less. Just hold her hand. Talk to her. Tell her all the things you'd want her to know. She won't be able to answer you, but she might hear and understand, and it might make it . . . easier. I'll just be out in the sitting room if you need me, if anything changes. . . ."

I nod and walk into the bedroom scented by that peculiar combination of incense, aromatic oil, medication, and disease. Sunshine streams in through an open curtain at the foot of the bed, and in it, a world of dust motes' microscopic life. Before I draw up the sagging armchair next to the bed, I study the woman for a long moment. She's outlined in golden light, and her face, her eyelids, seem papery and translucent. If it weren't for the faintest rise and fall of her chest, she might be an effigy.

I have no last words for her and I wish I did. If Lela were here now, what would she say? What would she do?

I don't know what comes over me—regret? grief?—but I place my left hand on Mrs. Neill's forehead; a gesture almost as old as mankind itself. Of benediction, of farewell.

The instant I touch her, my left hand begins to burn with a strange phantom pain. There's a building pressure behind my eyes as I flame into contact with the woman's very . . . *soul*.

And I see, I see—

Lela as a squalling newborn; vicious arguments between a younger Mrs. Neill and the man beside her in the dusty wedding photo I spied on the hallway table; Mrs. Neill and a toddler-size Lela in the backyard of a tiny blond-brick house by a railway line, the noise of the passing trains causing Lela to cover her ears and howl; Lela and her mother living in an apartment by the sea, with peeling wallpaper and water stains on the ceiling; the two of them walking hand in hand to Lela's elementary school; Mrs. Neill and a teenage Lela on a houseboat somewhere warm, arm in arm and truly happy for a passing instant; Mrs. Neill in a string of dead-end jobs—receptionist, postal worker, cleaner, telemarketer; Mrs. Neill welcoming Lela home from high school, then college, all the pride of those days still fierce in her now, like a fire, only banked; Mrs. Neill collapsing on the hallway carpet in grief the day the family doctor called to let her know that the stage-one cancer they thought they'd stopped in its tracks had metastasized in multiple locations and there was not a lot more they could do except to make her comfortable.

It could be seconds, it could be hours, later, that I snatch my hand away from the dying woman's skin; and the second I do, she takes a great choking breath and opens her eyes. There's fear and wonder in them. And she's once more present and herself in this room. In the world of the living.

"Georgia!" I call out. Panic in my voice.

I hear footsteps running down the hall.

"Lel," Mrs. Neill breathes, her eyes searching mine. "You're early."

"Karen?" Georgia exclaims, brushing past me to grasp Mrs. Neill's thin wrist in one hand, turning it over quickly to check the pulse. "You've come back to us."

She lays Mrs. Neill's hand gently on the bed moments later. "A steady one hundred and twenty beats per minute," she says incredulously, reaching for her patient's bedcovers. "How are you feeling? You gave us a scare."

Lela's mother waves one hand at the nurse, cutting her off.

"Your hand felt very warm, darling," she says to me tenderly, the words almost lost in the hum of machinery. "You're not taking ill with a summer flu?"

When I shake my head, she murmurs, "Do you remember that houseboat we chartered with the O'Connors and the Richardsons? On the Murray?"

I don't, of course. But I saw it in her mind and I nod.

"It was like we were there again. Remember how, when we came home, it felt for days afterward as if our beds had become boats themselves? We'd lie there, and it felt as if the waves were still rocking us to sleep. Our bodies had grown accustomed to the motion. Like we'd brought the river home inside us. We were happy then, weren't we? Really happy."

I nod again, and she whispers, "But it was more beautiful this time, Lel. There was light all around. The grass on the banks was so green, greener than it has any right to be, because it's never green along the Murray these days, is it? And I didn't feel any pain. You and I were like we are now, and we were leaning on the rails, looking out at the diamonds on the water, and I didn't want to leave, darling. I could have stayed that way forever, you and me, on that boat, just traveling. I didn't want to leave."

I think: *You almost didn't leave; you almost didn't come back.* And I wonder if *I* did that. If I somehow drew Lela's mother back to us again.

Georgia reaches for the covered cup of water on the bedside table, lifts it to Mrs. Neill's cracked lips, just to wet them, but Lela's mother waves her away again. She's all eyes, wild hair, jaundiced skin and bones. I wonder what kind it is, her cancer. But I can't ask because I should know.

"Too painful to swallow the last couple of days," she murmurs. "Won't be long now, Lel; then I won't be a burden to you anymore. . . ."

"Don't talk like that, Karen," Georgia scolds, then leaves the room to answer the doorbell that's just rung.

"Having you home, Lel, it's better than any drug," Mrs. Neill whispers, before losing consciousness again.

* * *

It's almost evening, and the neighbor, Bernadette, has come and gone. She cooked a nutritious meal for Mrs. Neill, which I put through the blender and tried to feed to her a spoonful at a time. But she wouldn't eat, said it hurt too much.

There was no point in my turning around and going back to the Green Lantern, so I told Georgia she could go too, that we wouldn't need anyone from the palliative care team overnight.

"You're sure you can cope?" she'd replied.

I could tell she was still unable to understand how she'd misread the signs. Mrs. Neill's sudden turnaround *knocked her for six*, as they say in this strange local idiom, making her question her own judgment.

The house is quiet now with just the two of us here. I want to head back out into the teeming, dirty world to find the answers I'm searching for, but if Georgia was right and Karen Neill is indeed at death's door, I don't want to be responsible for depriving her of her daughter's company in her last hours. I'm not that heartless. One more night can't hurt, can it?

When I come back from the bathroom, Lela's thick hair still damp, Mrs. Neill is asleep again. The sunlight piercing through the windows of the old house, warming the floorboards of her bedroom, striking sparks off the mirror, the walker, the mobile washstand, is the color of amber wine.

I sit cross-legged in the armchair beside the bed and watch Lela's mother sleep. The shadows begin to lengthen, and I am lost in thought when I feel a hand on my shoulder.

Faster than I would have believed possible, I half pivot in my seat to crush the intruder's wrist with my burning left hand—but it meets nothing but air.

I turn and look up into his face, and my animal fear turns to a kind of rapture. For suddenly he is with me again, in this room, love in his eyes. For *me*. The one who is so like Luc that he could be his brother, his blood. Save that he is mortal.

"Ryan," I whisper, as he pulls me into his arms. The knowledge of his name is almost reflexive, like something embedded at some murky, cellular level.

"You should see the look on your face. It's priceless," he teases as I tentatively place my cheek against his achingly familiar profile and breathe in his addictive, clean, male smell.

He's wearing a beat-up leather jacket, a faded navy T-shirt, scuffed boots, and blue jeans. And it feels so right, the two of us standing together like this.

I'm almost afraid of what I'm feeling, surging like a sea inside. What would Luc say if he knew? He's always been so . . . protective of me; though *protective* doesn't even begin to describe how carefully he watched me and watched over me. When he chose me for his own, that was how it was to be, forever and ever, *in saecula*. He made me feel safe. Made me the center of his world.

I am overwhelmed by a vision of Luc and me entwined in each other's arms within a bower of flowers, the air heavy with the fragrance of neroli, jasmine, white magnolia, orange blossom, a thousand different blooms that no human hand could possibly have put together. It was our place, the hanging garden he created for me alone. Seen since that day only in dreams, and likely gone forever.

"All I want," he'd said, resting his forehead against mine, "is your enduring happiness. You are the best and most loved thing in my life—let nothing ever be possible, or complete, if you are not with me. And may the elements witness my vow in all their silent glory."

The memory is so real that when I look up and see Ryan there in Luc's place, I feel the lines of my face collapse like crumpled paper. The pain is so intense, I wonder how I can feel this way and still be alive. But some traitorous part of me continues to react to Ryan's presence here, his touch, in a way I can't understand.

Ryan pulls me closer. "God, I've missed you. You have no idea how much. I've been in agony since you've been gone."

He looks down at me, smoothing back my hair with his hands. "They're fighting dirty this time. They actually managed to make you forget who I am. I didn't think it was possible to mess you up any more than They already have, but They did it. I'd congratulate Raph if I wasn't so angry with him I could *destroy* him."

I frown. There's something I'm missing in his words.

Ryan steps back, holding me at arm's length the better to look at me, really look at me. And I realize with a start that I'm standing here in my own body, my garments drifting around me—white, glowing, ghostly—though there is no breeze in the room. Beside me, Lela's sleeping form is curled up in the chair. I am myself, as I once was before I was cursed to roam the earth.

The truth hits me an instant later.

"This is a *dream*," I snarl. "When I wake, you'll be gone. And I won't remember you."

"You don't even remember 'me' now." Ryan laughs. "And I need you to remember. It's the first step."

And suddenly it's no longer Ryan with his arms around me, but Luc. It had been Luc all along.

"You're disappointed," he says, his expression curious, watchful.

"Of course not," I reply quickly. "How could I be? When it's only ever been you?"

Do I imagine that my voice falters a little as I say the words? Luc must not hear, for he spins me around lightly so that the room dissolves—in the way that dreams make possible—and I find that we are standing on a desolate beach under moonlight. It's a place I've seen before, through someone else's eyes. Deserted of any living thing except we two. The water is gray, tempestuous, with vast offshore waves, a dangerous reef out beyond the shallows, shaped like a devil's crown.

Despite the roaring wind coming off the water, whipping the sand through our hair, stinging against our skin, I hear Luc clearly when he murmurs, "What would it take to unlock the mystery of you?"

I shake my head, helpless to answer him, the elements outside a replica of what's inside me.

Lightning pierces the blanket of night around us, striking the distant water, lighting up the horizon, illuminating the stark coastline, the jagged rocks that rise up beyond the shallows like reaching fingers or claws, the lashing boughs of the trees that line the shore like a vast, crowding army of the undead.

"I haven't forgotten you." Luc breathes against my neck as the elements rage around us. "I haven't forgotten a single thing we said or did together. I'm obsessed by my memories of you. They're eating me alive. Why can't I find you? Why haven't you tried harder to find me?"

"Tried harder?" I cry. "You can't know what it's been like for me!"

"Or me," Luc growls. "When you . . . left me, it ruined *everything*."

I shiver, wanting the dream to be over, desperate to wake myself up. I try to pull myself out of his arms, but Luc's grip is suddenly like iron.

I begin to struggle and twist in earnest. "I don't

respond well to threats," I growl. "You, of all people, should know that about me."

Luc shakes me roughly. "Where are you?" he cries, as if I haven't spoken. "Answer me!"

"I don't know!" I wail. "I don't know."

He shakes me again, and the feeling in my heart turns to . . . anger.

A surge of fury breaks in me, higher than any wave. And my left hand begins to *burn*.

I draw breath sharply, contemplating the pale corona engulfing my hand, beginning to creep silently up my wrist, white, like ghost flame. How can something so beautiful be so . . . corrosive?

Luc's eyes gleam with an answering fire as he contemplates my evanescent skin. "That's the key," he hisses.

"Key?" I gasp, unable to flex the fingers of my left hand. The agony is leaching into my voice. Can he hear it? The flame is like a living thing. I see it throw out questing tendrils, as if it is sentient and seeking new sources of fuel.

"Fear and anger," he replies. "Fear and anger allow you to access your true nature, those powers that are yours by right. Fear and anger are a window upon your soul; shall lead you back to me. Fear and anger." He laughs, almost to himself. "It's only fitting."

I cannot look away from the steady conflagration of my flesh. My forearm is now wholly incandescent. It feels as if nothing will ever rival this *pain*.

"What of love?" I remind him sharply, my voice rising as the flame also rises. "It's a currency I would rather deal in."

"Love!" His voice is disdainful. "Love is what got us into this mess in the first place. The time for love will come again, but now is the time for *war*. If you won't look for me, then find that mortal boy, Ryan, return to the place where he lives, and I will come for you. But do it quickly—I have waited long enough."

"When you're like this," I whisper, "I don't even know you."

In answer, Luc shakes me again. "Stupid creature! Without him there will never again be an *us*. You will always and forever be just a lost girl. Ryan is only the first step of many that must be taken. Don't you understand? *Find him*."

With a roar of frustration fierce enough to shake

ancient bedrock, he suddenly streaks skyward with me in his arms, held fast, a living projectile.

And I remember . . . *my terrible fear of heights*—

The surface of the earth falling away from us at a speed that must surely be against the laws of nature; the vault of heaven looming until we break into the cold embrace of the eternal night sky, continue streaming away into absolute space, the airless, aching void. How is it we are able?

In dreams, anything is possible.

Yet it all feels so real that I cannot draw breath; terror is interfering with my musculature, my physiognomy.

Luc steers us madly, deliberately, at a piece of space junk the size of a small mountain—a rain of certain death were it to fall upon the earth—and smashes through it, laughing wildly. Though I cower and turn my face away within the circle of his embrace, the debris seems not to touch us.

This may be a dream, but dreams bring the truth to the surface, don't they? And I know now that I cannot bear to fly, because to fly might mean to fall. And yet we spiral deeper through the uncaring universe than anyone has ever been, and I wonder why I—why Luc, the one who loves me—would inflict a dream like this upon my sleeping consciousness. A dream as real, as terrifying, as this could bring death to someone like me.

I *know* Luc feels my fear, yet he does nothing but take us faster, higher, in loops, tailspins, and whorls through the vacuum-sealed cosmos. We scream past the echoes of dead and dying nebulae, speed through ancient echoes of light, dust, gas, and radiation as if such things have no power over us. I try to remember to breathe, but I'm so afraid, I feel light-headed, like I'm going to black out.

Luc tightens his already suffocating grip about me— and takes us *through* an asteroid as big as a fifty-story building.

For a moment we flow through the crystalline structure as if we have become reduced to our base particles—we are commingled with the very rock itself. It's as if we have become . . . *atomized*. Luc still himself, me still myself, separate but strangely blended, running through, between, facets of immovable stone. It is a sensation that is at once familiar and yet skin-crawling, extraordinary.

And as we emerge, whole and individual, from the other side of the spinning asteroid, my torso, my entire self, is engulfed in white flame, and I see—

A multitude of lives playing out before me; myriad existences that I have lived before and am somehow able to live again. Some terminate abruptly with the sense of something frustrated and unfinished; some go for years at a stretch. But then there's a sense of escalating dislocation, time seems to spool forward, and I see glimpses of—

Bloody unifications: the state of Qin? The fall of Samarkand? Troy is under siege; and Antioch and Jerusalem; the Huguenots are put to the sword before my eyes, the streets running with blood—all as if happening right now, in this moment, and not some long-lost yesterday. People run every which way around me, as ants would when under attack, and it occurs to me—even as I reel from the horrors I am witnessing—that men, like ants, engage in these same behaviors over and over again, wreaking senseless destruction upon each other through the generations. There is warfare on horseback, by ship, and by plane; there are crucifixions, beheadings, burnings, explosions, earthquakes, tsunamis, acts of genocidal madness, acts of God; there is death on a scale so large that I perceive the stars through a veil of blood, life *in extremis*, and I gasp, "Why are you showing me these things?"

"All this is your own doing," Luc replies. "Your own self's way of telling you that it is time to wake from the punishing nightmare, time to reclaim your true place at my side. Think of this as merely a . . . catalyst. It's all inside you—everything you need to know, everything you are capable of. It's still there."

I look at him wide-eyed. Could it be true? The power to reclaim my freedom, my identity, has been *in* me all this time?

Luc's arms are about me still, his chin resting atop my hair. "Memory is power . . . *Mercy.*"

He laughs as he utters the name I have given myself; and as he does, I am assailed with images of my life as Carmen Zappacosta.

There's a girl standing before me—once beautiful; now tiny, wasted, abused. I get a name—*Lauren?*

"Yes," Luc says, pleased.

There's a man, too. Tall, lean, also once beautiful . . . though now there are bleeding holes where his eyes should be, blood running from his ruptured ears, his mouth shaped forever in a scream.

Paul? I name this one hesitantly, shrinking from his image.

"Yes," Luc repeats, satisfaction in his voice. "Good."

For a singular moment—a breath suspended—Luc and I drift, still encircled in each other's arms, watching the stars wheel silently about us. Comets flare across the galaxies; the edges of the universe pulse and contract like a living organism, a beating heart. And it almost feels like the way it used to be. But then I remember the rage I saw in Luc's eyes, and I shiver.

I stare at his face, struggling to reconcile that look with the smile I see now playing on his lips. He's so beautiful that it's as if he's been touched by the sun itself, as if he carries some of its light with him always.

"Memory is power, Mercy," he says. "It shall restore you to yourself in the end."

As I look on with horror, Luc's beautiful features begin to twist into a parody of themselves, a fearful carnival mask. And then shatter—like glass, like a mirror breaking—and his image disintegrates.

I am alone again, screaming, *"No!"* A cry loud enough to shatter the fundamentals of a world.

And I am falling, falling, falling through the night sky. Burning earthward, like space junk wrenched out of orbit, like a fatal meteor, my screams rending the universe about me, the dream itself, into shreds.

I wake with a jolt in a girl's body, in a chair, in red plaid pajamas that are worn out at the knees, as if I have just, literally, fallen out of the sky. I am rigid with fear, and it takes me some time to work out where I am, who I am meant to be.

Finally, the beat of my borrowed heart begins to slow, my breathing grows easier, my sight grows clear once more. It's dawn. I can tell from the cool clear quality of the light, the stillness outside punctuated only by birdsong. We've just crossed the threshold into morning. Though it feels as if I've returned from a place so distant, I've crossed light-years to be back at Karen Neill's bedside.

She's asleep, still breathing, her condition unchanged from the night before.

I stare at the backs of Lela's hands, which are shaking a little. Turn them over, study the palms. So small, so ordinary. And yet . . . I can still almost feel a faint trace of fire in the fingers of her left hand.

I recall every moment of my dream, as if the fear and anger I felt were, indeed, a key to unlocking memories that my enemies would prefer remained hidden. For I know now why the Eight tried to make me forget my brief life as Carmen Zappacosta. They were trying to hide Ryan Daley, his feelings for *me*.

And I'm angry at myself, too—for allowing myself to forget someone so unforgettable in the first place. When I was Carmen, Ryan made me feel so much less alone; he treated me as an equal, like someone whose opinions actually mattered, like I was actually part of the life I was living, part of the family I was living with. I'll always be grateful to him for that. When I was with him, I felt like less of a . . . freak. I wanted to know more about him. Hadn't wanted to leave him, but had always known that I would have to, and it made every second we spent together that much more precious and sacred. Beyond that, I can't contemplate a future, an alternate universe, where someone like him and someone like me could be together in any way, shape, or form, so I'm just going to look at this the way Luc does—coldly, pragmatically—and try not to think about the other stuff, the human stuff.

You're not a human, I tell myself fiercely. *So stop behaving like one. All you have to do is find Ryan and wait it out. That's all. Feelings can be put aside. You've done worse.*

And I know it for a truth.

I rise unsteadily and head to the kitchen.

Maybe it *is* all inside me, everything I need to get the real me back, but I'm like someone who has to relearn how to walk, talk, eat. The connections are missing, or badly compromised. And I have so much lost ground to cover. But I'm a quick study. I'm awake now, more than I have ever been before. Body and soul are beginning to synchronize. Overnight, something in me has begun to regenerate, to lay down new wiring.

The blockages inside me are dissolving, so that I remember, too, how, when I was Carmen, I *was* able to call on unexpected powers that I still can't explain. Like how if I'm ticked off enough, I have the ability to hurt people with my bare hands.

Paul's eyes? His ears? *I* did that. The knowledge makes me go cold inside.

I study the refrigerator door and locate the telephone number, cross to the wall phone to dial it. The woman who answers promises that a member of the palliative care team will be over shortly.

I hurry down the hallway to Lela's bedroom, dig a random T-shirt out of a pile of clothes lying on a chair, put it on. Pull on a pair of shorts. It's like I'm color-blind—the top's sky blue; the shorts are pumpkin-colored, baggy, and ill-fitting. But I don't care. I know what I have to do now, and it's as if a fire has been lit within.

I wait impatiently for a kind-faced woman called Abby to arrive and help out until Georgia can get here.

"Georgia brought me up to speed on what happened yesterday," Abby whispers as she sets down her medical kit near Mrs. Neill's bed. "We'll call you if there's any change."

I practically fly down the path, feel like vaulting the fence. Want to grab the steering wheel out of the bus driver's nicotine-stained fingers so that we ignore all the stops, all the angry people, and reach the city faster.

Because Luc's got it so right. He can't find me, and I've had a lousy time trying to find him, but Ryan Daley is *mortal*. He has a physical body and a physical location. I've touched the guy, broken bread with him, called his cell phone, even stayed at his home. Met his parents, for Christ's sake, and his bitch of an ex-girlfriend. He lives in a small town called Paradise, on a coastline somewhere; the ugliest place you're ever likely to see, a complete misnomer. But that's the point: there can't be too many places like it. Even though most days I couldn't tell you where I am, or where I've been, I know I can find it again.

Luc, on the other hand, I've never seen outside the realms of sleep, in this century or the last. I've lost count of how many years it's been since we were in the same place together, flesh *and* spirit. I've never been able to track him down, not even after all this time, not even after all the hints he keeps dropping, like crumbs from a benevolent god. Until I began to fathom what had happened to me, I'd taken Luc for a figment of my diseased imagination, a recurring dream, a vision of glory sent to disturb my rest.

Though there are still holes in my recall big enough

to steer a whole fleet of cruise ships through, maybe some things are finally beginning to . . . stick. Because something happened to me last night. Whatever it is that keeps me this way—caged inside another; doomed to play the ghost in the machine—something changed when I saw Ryan Daley in my dreams.

And what's more, none of the Eight, not even Luc himself, has any idea of the extent to which I'm *back*. I'm remembering *more* than the jumbled handful of memories Luc fed me: like the internal layout of Ryan's house and how it had felt sitting beside him in his car. Like the way Carmen's cell phone screen *looked* when I dialed Ryan's number, digit by digit. I have his number. *I remember Ryan's number*.

I'm feeling something I haven't felt in a long time. Hope so raw, it's akin to pain.

Lela's boss, Mr. Dymovsky, is behind the till this morning, and I nod in his direction before throwing myself into the breakfast rush. I'm more brusque than usual as I bag the orders and shovel them out in a steady stream. Even Reggie's in awe of the way I'm handling the jerks and losers, the downtrodden women and born-to-rule types that filter in here looking for sustenance.

Maybe I'm overdoing it, allowing too much of my own personality to shine through, because Mr. Dymovsky says shrewdly in his Russian-accented English, "Maybe you forget to take care of yourself. Something about you, about your face, looks different, I think? Thinner, maybe. Sharper. You up to this? Because if you not, I find another girl to do the job, okay? Because we no need another Reggie here. One Reggie, she's plenty."

He's a perceptive man, Dmitri Dymovsky, which you'd never know if you simply took him at face value. Because who would ever wear a cartoon tie with a striped, short-sleeved shirt? And the way he's tucked both into the waistband of a pair of tight brown slacks gives him the profile of a boiled egg. He has wispy gray hair that seems to be trying to float off his head, a thin mustache, and big pouches under his pale blue eyes. He might be anywhere between fifty-five and seventy-five. He looks like a kind fool. But to misjudge him would be a mistake. I like him.

"Sorry, Mr. Dymovsky," I say as I slap together bacon and egg on a roll with lettuce; bacon and egg on a roll with cheese; bacon and egg on a roll, hold the barbecue sauce. "I'll tone it down."

"Good girl," he says mildly. "Oh, and Lela, next time wear black, okay?"

I nod like I mean it, but I've got one eye on the door the whole time, waiting for Ranald to arrive.

Mr. Dymovsky puts on a battered straw fedora, lifts it in our direction, then calls out as he leaves that he's heading to the market to do his weekly shopping for bargain tomatoes, small goods, cheese, lettuce, and fruit by the boxload.

At 10:42, like clockwork, Ranald bats aside the sticky plastic curtain and practically falls through the front door with his laptop bag, too-big suit jacket, and his serious expression. It's 10:45 on the dot by the time he sets up his computer, and Cecilia slides the first heart-starter of the day his way. Time for me to get what I came for: information.

When I walk up to his table, Ranald closes the window he's working on and smiles. "Did you want me to find out more about Carmen Zappacosta for you?"

I shake my head. "The focus of my inquiry has shifted slightly. I need to find Ryan Daley, the brother of the abductee. I need to contact him in person, but all I have is a cell phone number. Find him for me and I'll be in your debt forever."

"You mean that?" Ranald says, surprise and eagerness warring in his expression. "I'm going to hold you to it—dinner and a movie if I get you what you want."

"Deal," I shoot back, not intending to stick around long enough to have to go through with anything. This time it's about *me*. It's my time now, and if I have to climb over the bodies of lovelorn IT guys to get the answers I'm seeking, then so be it.

Ranald types Ryan's name into the search engine and gets ten pages of results. He shakes his head, unwilling to wade through random fishing blogs and *Heavy Metal's All-time Greatest Hits* lists generated by schmucks called Ryan Daley.

"Let's narrow it down a little more," he says. "Cell phone number?"

I give it to him, and feel a jolt when my eyes settle on the first item that comes up on the first page of new results.

"What is that?" I breathe, leaning in closer to the screen and running my finger along the string of letters and numbers beneath Ryan's name and his cell phone number.

Ranald's voice is dismissive. "It's the URL for his

page on a social networking website for show ponies, fake friends, and stalkers. How do you know this guy again?"

I almost can't speak for the sudden rapid pounding of Lela's heart in my ears. "Someone I lost contact with. An old friend that I've been meaning to look up for a long time, but the whole Carmen thing flared up. He should be a lot more . . . receptive to hearing from me now."

Ranald looks at me suspiciously.

"That's why I need the background info you dug up," I say hastily. "I had to know if I had the right guy, and I do. Can you . . . click on this?"

"Sure," he says, lips pursed as if the action is distasteful.

A Web page fills the screen almost instantly, with a heart-stopping photo of Ryan in the top left corner. It's a moody black-and-white shot, and he's looking away from the camera, but I'd know the planes of his face, the curve of his mouth, that fall of black hair, anywhere.

Just seeing him again like this brings back the sound of his voice, the way he holds a steering wheel, the way

I wanted to hold his hand but didn't trust myself to, because my getting involved with someone like him—where would it lead?

The page asks politely if I would like to add Ryan Daley as a friend or send Ryan Daley a message. I feel a surge of the sea that I carry around inside.

"You found him," I say, placing my hands on Ranald's shoulders in gratitude. "You found him."

My defenses are down, as they always seem to be where Ryan is involved. So I'm unprepared when Ranald takes his hands off the keyboard and places them over mine, where they rest on his shoulders. Before I have the sense to rip my hands away, I see, I see—

A dead bird nailed to a tree by its wings. A taunting circle of young male faces, fists raised, mouths wide, screaming obscenities, screaming at me to "Do it! Do it!"

Small, shrieking rodents set alight in their cages.

The hard, stained, porcelain rim of a bathroom sink rushing up to meet me as if I'm falling or I've been pushed.

A battered cat strung up by its tail, a crossbow bolt through its ravaged body.

The surface of someone's hairy, giant fist the moment before the world turns Technicolor with pain—

I break contact abruptly, and the images leave me, and I can no longer hear the roar of male aggression or smell the winter air, the scent of smoke and gas, feel the dry crunch of leaf litter and gravel under my feet, or feel the fear, the terrible fear.

"Jesus God, Ranald," I say raggedly. "Don't ever touch me again."

I'm shaking, but he doesn't need to know why. Nor do I need to know why he carries such things around in his head, like surface scum. I hate being touched; but this? This was something else altogether. I feel . . . dirty for witnessing something I was never supposed to see.

"I'm sorry," Ranald says, crossing his arms and blinking rapidly. "I don't know why I did that. I hope you didn't take it the wrong way."

For a moment, I think he's talking about the atrocities I saw in his mind that are somehow connected to his childhood. They *were* wrong. What other way could I take them? But then I realize he's talking about grabbing hold of Lela's hands, and the tenderness of that act belies the things I saw through his eyes. Maybe that's what boys do—hurt things that are smaller and more defenseless than they are. I wouldn't know. In the wider scheme of human history, are the things in Ranald's head so heinous?

I look at the image of Ryan Daley and feel Lela's heart leap again. I push the feel of human fist pounding human flesh, the hideous squealing of the tortured animals, the smell of burning flesh and fur, to one side. I still need Ranald's help, and I'm not prepared to wait until the next time a man bearing a laptop comes my way—which could be never—so I can't afford to be judgmental. A telephone on its own is no use to me right now; I know because I dialed Ryan's number this morning before I left Lela's house—the number I'd memorized when I was Carmen Zappacosta—and all I got was a prerecorded woman's voice telling me to *Please check the number before trying again.* I need access to this seething universe, this Internet, that is wholly manmade, and Ranald can provide that. I just need him to show me how it's done, and I can take it from there.

If Ranald's *sweet* on Lela, I can milk that. But carefully; I don't want to mix Lela up in something she can't back out of later. Engage, get what I want, disengage. I can be ruthless that way.

I pull my fractured thoughts together and reply as calmly as I can manage. "Of course I didn't take it the wrong way, Ranald. And I shouldn't have touched you either. It was inappropriate. Overly familiar. I apologize."

I hope he's hearing me, because it works both ways, buddy.

"You don't need to apologize," he says, relieved, and gestures for me to sit down in the seat beside him.

I remain standing.

"Look," he coaxes, "you don't own a computer, right?"

I shake my head.

"Tell you what. I'll set up a profile for you and you can message the guy. You choose the password, everything. I'll just fix you up and step away."

I drift in a little closer, watching as he clicks on a couple of icons. Ranald fills in Lela's first and last name, her gender, and makes up a birthday when I decline to provide him with one, his hands flying across the keyboard.

He stands and pushes the laptop across the table in my direction. "I'll let you fill in the e-mail address and password," he says. "So that you know everything's private and aboveboard."

He knows it's an offer I won't be able to refuse. He can tell from the way I can't take my eyes off the machine, how every line of my body seems to yearn toward it.

As if to underscore his words, he grabs his empty coffee mug and heads toward the service area. "Give me another double espresso, Cecilia," I hear him say.

"But it's too early for your second coffee, Mr. Kilkery," she says. "You always say you like you routine. You sure you want right now?"

I sit down in front of the laptop and stare at the keyboard, then back at the screen, where Lela's name is already filled in, the cursor blinking at me from the e-mail line.

From across the room, Ranald says, "Don't use your own name, birth date, telephone number, or home address as a password, Lela. They're too easy to crack."

Easy for him to say. Some of that information is locked away in Lela's brain. I wouldn't have the faintest idea how to access them, let alone type them in here.

When I continue to sit there unmoving, Ranald comes back with his double espresso. His distance is deliberate and respectful, but his tone is slightly incredulous. "You don't have an e-mail address, do you?"

I look up at him, and I'm sure he sees bewilderment in Lela's eyes, because he says quickly, "How about I just fill mine in there, and you can change it later, when you create an account for yourself? There are plenty of free webmail providers, it's no big deal."

Jargon, jargon, jargon. He lost me after *create*.

He spins the laptop his way and types a string of numbers and letters, moving the cursor onto the *Create Password* slot when he's done. Then he slides the machine back under my nose.

"Now, this *really* is something you can take care of on your own," he says. "Promise I won't look. Just a word, or a word with numbers. Or just numbers. Something that's meaningful to you that won't make sense to anyone else. It's to prevent people like me from seeing what you get up to online."

He laughs and walks away again, says to Cecilia, "Give me one of those salmon cakes, would you? Hold the sweet chili sauce."

I raise Lela's right hand uncertainly, puzzling at the letters in front of me, then type with one finger: *misericordia*. A row of twelve dots appears there in place of the actual letters. *Misericordia*: Latin for *mercy*—get it? The play on words brings a small smile to my lips. It's an in-joke for an audience of one.

"All done?" Ranald says, wiping his mouth with the back of his hand. "Then just click *Sign Up* and you're on your way."

I do what he asks and am faced with a "security question."

"What does it want now?" I almost howl. "Why is this taking so long?"

Ranald rolls his eyes and flaps one hand at me. "Move over, you Luddite," he snorts. "Let's do the rest of this together or I'll never get back to work. Some of us are expected to save the world, you know, day in, day out, one firewall application at a time."

I shift across to the other seat, and he slides himself in front of the machine. He types and clicks, types and clicks.

"Who do you want to add as a friend?" he says.

I'm struggling to keep the impatience out of my

voice as I peer at the screen. "I just want to send Ryan a message. I want to be able to talk to him right now. Is that possible with this"—I use the word hesitantly— "website?"

Ranald nods. "You can even see if the guy's online. We'll check in a minute."

He quickly adds himself as a friend before pausing at the *Profile* screen. "School, uni, employer?" he asks.

I look at him blankly, and he sighs and types *Green Lantern Café, Melbourne, Australia* beside the word *Employer*.

"You're not giving me a whole lot to work with here," he says cheerfully. "But I can see that you're about to explode with impatience, so let's get you a profile picture and you can send that message."

"You want a picture of me?" I wail softly. "Where do I get one of those?"

I feel as if Ryan and I are a heartbeat apart, like there's a gossamer veil between us that I can almost reach up and rip down, but the mechanics and minutiae of "connecting" with him are taking too long. I want to pick up that stupid machine and throw it to the ground with an anger so sudden and fierce that my left hand begins to ache. I jam it beneath my right armpit in quiet agony.

"No sweat," Ranald chuckles, misreading my expression of pain for one of impatience. "I can take a photo of you with the webcam in my laptop and upload it right now."

He turns the screen toward me again. "Smile for the birdie," he says, tapping his finger against a small lens built into the top of the screen. I hitch up the corners of Lela's mouth unconvincingly, exposing her uneven front teeth.

Ranald clicks through a couple of extra functions as the manic grin on my face fades away. "Done," he says, with satisfaction.

And just like that, the photo's taken and Ranald has uploaded it onto the profile page he's created for me. *Welcome, Lela Neill* is emblazoned across the top. Lela's face and head of cropped, brown-red hair fill the entire image, with only a thin corona of brilliant light behind them; I must have moved when the image was captured. She looks blurry and young and naïve. Exactly the opposite of the way I feel inside.

"We're in business," Ranald says.

I lower my hand, which no longer aches, and lean forward, excitement flaring. "Just find him again," I say impatiently.

Ranald performs a few functions, and Ryan's profile fills the screen once more. "Send him a message now, if you like. Take all the time you need," he says, and wanders away to engage Cecilia in further conversation.

The world shrinks down to the screen before my eyes. The noise of the refrigeration units and the industrial-strength kitchen fan, the passing traffic, a nearby construction site, all fade away.

I study what's written on Ryan's page, which isn't a whole lot: his birthday, what he thought of some movie he saw last night. I see that he has two hundred and seventy-one friends, and I mirror Ranald's actions, moving my finger along the touch-sensitive rectangle at the base of the keyboard, to be taken to page after page of profile photos and names. Good-looking teens, moody teens, a smattering of adults in family shots, wearing matching sweaters; people signified by cartoons, obscurely posed objects, or humanoid-shaped blobs.

I see that Brenda Sorensen is there, Ryan's ex-girlfriend. Richard Coates, Lauren Daley's boyfriend at the time she was snatched right out of her bedroom. It doesn't surprise me that Lauren herself isn't there, after what she's been through. I wonder how she's doing—if you ever really come back sane from something like that.

I click the *Back* button until I'm staring at Ryan's photo again, and find myself hunched over a little, shivering, arms crossed over my belly as if I'm in pain. My left hand no longer hurts, but the feeling inside is like acid running through my veins, instead of blood.

Still, I hesitate. I'm not a member of Ryan's tribe. I could be any old psycho out there in the world who's chanced across his picture.

I move my finger along the sliver of touch-sensitive steel, and the small arrow drifts erratically toward the *Send Message* option. I click on it finally, and a small window opens, Ryan's image in the top left-hand corner.

I'm no typist, but I'm a fast study. I scan the keyboard before me and tap into the window:

Ryan, it's Mercy. Don't look at the photo for clues. There's no connection between Lela or Carmen. No rationale for why she was chosen, and not by me. Never by me. I'm still the random by-product of some process I don't understand.

But I remember Lauren, I remember the pine tree you wasted, Mulvaney's, the drive out to

Little Falls, to Port Marie, in your car. All of it. Don't ask me how, but I do.

I'll find you. You know I'm nothing if not stubborn. Just tell me where you are, and quickly.

I add:

I need to go off-road for a while. There interested parties I need to avoid.

I click *Send*, and the words and the window instantly vanish, leaving only Ryan's profile page, that heart-stopping photograph in which he is looking away from me.

9

I sit there for a few minutes flicking between his window and my window. There's no change to either.

I add Ryan as a friend. Still nothing happens.

Ranald wanders back over, clearing his throat politely just in case I hadn't seen him coming. "All done?" he asks hesitantly, lifting the chewed fingernails of one hand to his lips, then remembering and dropping them again. "I do actually kind of need to get back to work now. Without me, P/2/P would fall apart. I personally wrote most of their applications—they'd be nothing without me, even though I get treated like the company punching bag most days. I keep threatening to leave, but no one ever takes me seriously." He gives a small self-deprecating laugh.

"Of course. I'm sorry," I say, and get up, disappointed that I can't linger over the machine, disheartened by the fact that Ryan didn't reply right away.

I mean, what was I expecting? I don't even know where he is. He could be asleep. He could be out of town.

Or with Brenda Sorensen, points out that little voice inside.

Now that Lauren's back safely, Ryan is free to get on with his life. I know Brenda wanted him back pretty badly, and what Brenda wants, Brenda usually gets. Ryan may take one look at the message sent to him by a total stranger from Melbourne, Australia, and hit *Delete*. There's no guarantee he'll even read it.

Despite all that, I'm hoping he'll see the message, understand it, and act on the feelings he had for me. He has to, or Luc and I might never "reconnect" again. There's a lot riding on this.

And truth be told, I'm kind of sick of having to be self-sufficient and resourceful, you know? It'd be nice to have someone in my corner, for a change; to be appreciated—loved, even—for myself, no matter what face I might be wearing. I'm the first one to tell you that self-pity is for idiots, but I wasn't made to bear these burdens alone. I was part of something bigger than me, once. I was made for a purpose, and, in some way, I know that I've failed.

I want to come in from the cold. I don't want to be an exile anymore. And if there are consequences, then so be it.

I catch myself drawing one finger down the side of Ryan's face on the screen, and hastily close the window.

"Sorry," I say again, hoping Ranald didn't catch my moment of weakness. "And thank you. You've been very generous with your equipment, and your time."

Ranald stares down at me for a moment. "You take care out there," he says quietly, tapping one ragged fingernail on the screen, which has now turned black. "It's called *the Web* for good reason. Newbies like you can get eaten alive."

"Thanks for the tip," I reply.

As I move out of my seat, I push the screen down toward the keyboard, thinking to close the machine.

"Wait!" Ranald exclaims. "Let me shut it down properly first."

I thought it had already turned itself off, but as I watch, a thin ribbon of white appears in the inky background of the screen, so faint that at first I think it's just a trick of the light. It streams toward me in a hypnotic, sidewinding fashion, like a cobra preparing to strike. As it expands and grows brighter, I see that it isn't a snake at all, but a quote in stark white text on that field of black.

It reads: *Abyssus Abyssum Invocat*—literally, *Hell Invokes Hell*. I frown. In common speech, I suppose you could say it means something like *One bad thing begets another*.

Before Ranald can catch me staring, I look away, and he sends his laptop to sleep, shutting it with a snap.

I give him a small wave, my gaze colliding with Sulaiman's as he stares out through the serving hatch, an unreadable expression on his face.

As soon as I leave here today, I'm going to that Internet place in Chinatown to see whether Ryan has responded to my message. I don't know if I can wait that long, or what I'll do if he does reply. How do I get from here to where he is? Lela's got no money, and I can hardly materialize there again, like I did once before. It doesn't work that way, no matter how much I might wish it to.

First step hardly even describes the journey I may have to make to get back to Luc.

And what happens to Lela's dying mother if Lela suddenly vanishes off the face of the earth? Because that's what I intend to do. I can't just abandon Karen Neill to save myself, can I?

But there's no point obsessing about any of this until I know if Ryan cares enough about me, Mercy, to reply. It all comes down to him. What he does next will determine the course of everything for me.

A customer blocks my way as I head back to the counter. It's the corporate gnome from yesterday morning who called Justine a hooker—probably back to settle a score with me. Well, get in line, I think.

Aloud, I say, "Can I help you?"

I know it's a warm day outside, but that can't possibly explain why the gnome is sweating as if he's in the grip of a terrible fever. His skin is slick and shiny with moisture, his thinning hair, mustache, and beard are dark with sweat, although the air conditioner is on full blast, as are the two ceiling fans. The man's eyes are wide, a blank terror in them. He looks wired.

He reaches out for my arm like a zombie, and it's instinctive when I reply sharply, "Don't touch me. What do you want?" in almost the same breath, the words running together.

"I want you to sit down," he says in a weirdly controlled voice. "And you, and you too." He swings and points a shaking finger at Sulaiman, at Cecilia behind the coffee machine. "Get out here."

Cecilia and I exchange glances before she slides around the counter and comes to an uncertain standstill in front of the hot food counter.

"You," he addresses Reggie, who's just come bustling into the café, swinging a couple of shopping bags. "Lock the door and put up the *Closed* sign. No one comes in or goes out."

"Now just a minute!" Ranald blusters, computer bag on one shoulder, on the verge of leaving. "I'm already late."

"Sit," says the gnome, stabbing one finger at a table near the door.

It's clear from Ranald's face that he hates being told what to do. But, responding to something in the man's voice, he reluctantly slides into a seat and places his computer bag between his feet.

Reggie takes the fight right up to the guy. "Franklin Murray, *I know who you are.* You buy a chicken salad sandwich from me almost every day. Which doesn't entitle you to do shit, in my book, let alone pull this kind of stunt."

Something in Reggie's waspish tone seems to harden the teetering resolve inside Franklin Murray's soul. Because suddenly the terror is gone and his face grows pale and set. He roars, loud enough to make Reggie lose her grip on one of her bags in surprise. "I want you all to SIT DOWN. WHY WON'T YOU SIT DOWN?"

"I'll call the cops," Reggie snaps, brassy to the last, hooking up the fallen shopping bag by one of its handles. "Don't push me."

"Don't push ME," Franklin screams, shaking bunched fists at Reggie like an apoplectic dwarf. "Don't ever push me again, you hard-faced bitch of a woman. Because I have a *gun.*"

He pulls it out of the inner breast pocket of his suit jacket and points it at my temple.

Reggie takes one look at the weapon and quietly shuts and locks the door, and turns the sign to read *Closed.*

"Pull down all the blinds," Franklin orders.

Reggie does as she's told without even a hint of back talk. He waves his gun at her, and she sits at an empty table, shopping bags abandoned in the aisle near the door.

"You!" Franklin addresses Sulaiman rudely. "You deaf as well as stupid? Get in here with the rest of them."

Sulaiman complies, but takes his time. He doesn't look afraid; in fact, he's showing no emotion at all. He's like a man mountain, broad and well over six feet tall. The man with the handgun doesn't clear five and a half.

"SIT," Franklin yells at him.

"I would prefer to stand," Sulaiman rumbles, wiping his hands on his apron, then tugging his cap off his head of short, black curls.

"I'll hit her," Franklin threatens, indicating me with the muzzle of the gun.

Sulaiman glances sharply at me before pulling out a chair and sinking into it carefully. It creaks as he pushes it back to give himself more legroom. He tosses his cap onto the table as if he is throwing down a challenge.

Satisfied, Franklin marches me back over to the seat I'd only just vacated and pushes me down into it. And that's when I feel it. That hot-cold, hair-raising energy that sets up a hum deep in my bones.

I look for the source of the feeling, see an errant patch of light moving across the wall near the air conditioner, see it fly across the face of the coffee machine a second later and get lost in the lit-up hot-food display and in the reflective chrome of the chair legs and seat backs.

The *malakh* is inside the room with us. The real world, the other world, quietly, imperceptibly, bleeding into each other once again.

Franklin waves his gun at Cecilia without speaking, and she slides into an empty chair, crossing her arms protectively around herself.

"What are you planning to do to us?" Ranald calls out. "People are going to miss me, you know. You chose the wrong guy to mess with."

"Oh yeah? You look like a low-level functionary to me," Franklin shoots back, and Ranald's expression darkens into fury for a moment. "I want you to pray, that's what I want you to do. Because I'm going to kill every single one of you and then I'm going to kill myself. That will show them."

"Show who?" I ask, and the black, single-barreled handgun swings back in my direction.

Out of the corner of my eye I watch a smudge of

light settle on the floor at Ranald's feet, slide onward a moment later, pool beneath the table at which Cecilia is seated.

The *malakh* is so close now that the energy it gives off is almost painful. The grating zing-zing noise it makes every time it moves is vibrating in my bones.

"Why are you doing this?" I say into the barrel of Franklin's gun, more curious than afraid. "What would drive you to destroy a room full of strangers? Or yourself?"

I don't believe for a second that he means to do it. I don't need to touch him to know that he's literally oozing fear. He's a coward and a braggart. He'll never pull the trigger. On me *or* himself. The man's just looking for a spot on the nightly news, crying out for some good old-fashioned attention.

"I poured my blood into that company." Franklin's voice begins to shake, along with his gun hand. "And they 'rationalized' my job out of existence. *I'm fifty-two years old.* My wife"—he's openly weeping now, tears streaming down his cheeks, into his beard, snot running down his face—"will not remotely understand when I tell her that I will be forced to declare bankruptcy. She buys a new wardrobe for each goddamned *season*. She will not comprehend it when I tell her that we are on the brink of losing *everything*."

I frown, watch the blur of light leach slowly across the floor. Settle almost up against one of Franklin's shiny Italian loafers.

"I'm going to make them pay—in blood," the little man sobs.

"You will be in Hell, Franklin," Sulaiman warns from his chair.

"SHUT UP!" Franklin yells. "I didn't ask for your opinion, darkie. There's no such place as Hell."

"It's not just a place," Sulaiman answers, undeterred. "It's a state. And your soul will be lost to it immediately if you do what you say you intend."

The little puddle of light seems to shiver, to lift partway off the greasy linoleum, at Sulaiman's words.

"Do you want me to shoot you first?" Franklin shrieks, peeling the gun off of me and pointing it at Sulaiman. "Because I will. I'm not here for a lesson in theology from someone like you." He spits on the ground.

"You wouldn't know the first thing about someone like me," Sulaiman answers gravely.

Franklin cocks the hammer of the gun with the thumb of his right hand and steps backward into the pool of light at his feet.

In the strange manner I sometimes have of taking in too much too quickly, I register in an instant that the light is gone. *Gone into Franklin Murray.*

Franklin begins to claw wordlessly at his corded neck with his free hand as the *malakh* takes possession of his body. "I . . . can't . . . breathe," he gasps, eyes bulging. He seems to be dancing on the spot to some crazy beat that only he can hear. The *malakh*'s power must be weakening, because Franklin's actually trying to fight it off.

I see Reggie shoot a look across the room at Cecilia. Wide-eyed, Ranald is watching the little man scratch his face, his torso.

Franklin's skin is giving off that sickly gray glow now, although no one in the room but me seems to notice.

"Give me the gun, Franklin," Sulaiman says, with narrowed eyes. "You don't want to do this."

His words have the opposite effect. In a state beyond rage, beyond reason, Franklin pulls the trigger.

Do I imagine that I hear the firing pin striking the primer, the explosion of some unstable compound within, the roar of a secondary ignition, the cartridge leaving the chamber? Do I imagine that I react in the same moment that the bullet enters the barrel, surging out of my chair and pushing the man's gun hand upward with my left hand as my right reaches toward his face?

I wonder where my anger has gone. It's been replaced by a terrible sadness, a bone-deep weariness. There is so much desperation in this world, played out at the margins, hardly disturbing the surface.

The instant the heel of my hand touches Franklin's forehead, I see—

Everything that is running through his head, in Technicolor. The face of his exacting wife, coldly beautiful, expensively maintained; the memory of when each son was born, both now in their late teens, both taking after their brunette mother in looks, in attitude, with their constant want, want, *want*; the first dog Franklin ever owned; the funeral of the first person he ever knew to die; a marketing presentation where the audio system failed, leaving him speechless before an audience of hundreds; his first promotion; an argument with his father that resulted in blows and a rift that never healed; the moment he was fired and told to clear his desk out within the hour. There's his fear, too, that he might be suffering some kind of stroke, some kind of seizure. Just a jumble of ordinary things; his life reduced to mere seconds, mere flashes; a sound-and-light show amped up by adrenaline, by the belief that he will shortly depart this world and it will all have been for nothing.

I sense, too, the *malakh*'s misery, pain, and rage as it uses Franklin as the blunt instrument of its wrath, fighting me for control of the gun.

I want to die! it shrieks inside my mind. *Why won't you let me die?*

Weak as it is, the creature has amplified Franklin's physical strength by a thousandfold, and I almost cannot hold him back as I reply into the space behind his eyes: *This is not the way. We cannot be killed by bullets; we cannot be killed by weaponry. The body may perish, but the spirit will live on, wounded, twisted, marked by what it has seen and done. Our kind may only kill and be killed by each other. Set the gun down, leave him. This is not the way.*

The three of us are locked in a physical struggle for what seems an eternity.

Though, it can't be, can it? Because it all happens in the time it takes for a gun to fire, for me to deflect the man's firing arm away, for a bullet to lodge itself harmlessly in the ceiling above our heads.

As Franklin tries to pull the trigger again, the *malakh* howling and raging behind his eyes, I snarl into his face trying to reach him: "*Mors ultima linea rerum est*, Franklin. Death is everything's final limit. If you do this, there will be no turning back. You condemn more than just yourself. Those children of yours; that wife you're so terrified of failing? You end your life, then you also end theirs as they know it. It all changes in the instant. Make something more of the present, you fool."

The gun we're grappling over is hot to the touch and wreathed in the smell of cordite and death. I feel the *malakh* as a tornado inside Franklin, clinging on grimly to his living body. It doesn't seem as if either of them can really hear me, both are so wounded and empty. They seem unaware of their dingy surroundings—or the five other people in the café that Franklin chose to take as prisoners on a random, sunny summer's morning.

Without knowing why or how, I roar into the space inside Franklin's head: *Exorcizo te!*

And there is a blinding flash of light, brighter than

magnesium when it burns, brighter than lightning come down to earth. So brief that no one in the Green Lantern takes it for more than a flash of sunlight. But I know what it is. And I know that it's gone, the *malakh* is gone. Gone back into the wide and pitiless world, to wander without respite.

10

Franklin drops his gun arm, drops the gun, racked by
heaving sobs. I lift my right hand from his brow, let my
left fall gently to my side.

He doesn't look at me as he wails, "I'm sorry, I'm so
sorry. I don't know what came over me."

Still weeping, he bends and wrestles the fallen gun
back inside his breast pocket, then unlocks the front
door and bats his way through the plastic curtain, leaving the café as unceremoniously as he'd entered it.

Sulaiman gives me a long, level look and glances
down at his watch. "It is time to pray," he says, standing up and heading for the kitchen. "Time to give
thanks to God, unbelievers, for you have been spared.
For now."

The kitchen door swings shut behind him, and Reggie, Ranald, and Cecilia look at one another, at me, with white faces.

Ranald staggers out the door, hugging his computer bag. Not cocky or composed now. No.

He is followed in short order by Cecilia and Reggie, who each grab a hodgepodge of personal items and leave without saying when or whether they'll be back.

I'm in the mood to talk. Near-death experiences can do that to you, I find. But there's suddenly no one left to talk to.

I head into the kitchen, where Sulaiman is calmly rolling out a prayer mat and listening to tinny, Arabic-sounding music on a portable radio.

I don't know where the words come from, but I say, "This is the *salah* that you are doing? The ritual prayer?"

He nods. "That is the name some give it."

I don't think I've ever witnessed a devout Muslim at prayer before, and I'm fascinated by the stillness and devotion in Sulaiman's face. For one so large, he moves near silently as he folds his frame down upon the colorful mat he has placed in one tiled corner of the cluttered, greasy kitchen.

I lean against the wall near the portable red fire extinguisher and the ragged poster that exhorts all who read it to *Wash Your Hands!* "I should think there would be an extra element of gratitude today in your prayers."

"What came to pass was already within His contemplation," Sulaiman says, his dark eyes flicking up to meet mine for an instant. "And so no 'extra' thanks need be given. It has simply occurred."

I shake my head and walk toward the swinging door. "Fatalist," I say, good-naturedly, though it's meant as a kind of insult.

"Blasphemer," Sulaiman shoots back from his position on the mat, forehead to the ground.

I pause at the door. "I know plenty of . . . people like you. Who have an unwavering belief that every step in the narrow, bitter little lives of people like Franklin Murray is preordained and inescapable, that free will does not come into it. If things really *are* preordained, and I hadn't stepped in to save you, then you might be dead now."

Sulaiman exhales. "Ah, but your act itself—was it not preordained? What sets you apart from any of us?

Do not speak to me of 'free will,' for we will never see eye to eye. My God is a jealous god. His will prevailed, as it always does."

I glare down at his broad back. "I like to think that I'm of all faiths rather than just one in which choice appears to form no part of the equation."

Though, if truth be told, I am so blank inside that I don't recall the tenets of my particular belief system, or whether I even have one.

Sulaiman raises himself onto his knees and gives me a challenging stare. "No," he says slowly. "I see into your heart, and I see that you are a person of no faith, and that is how you have come to be here. Now leave me," he says dismissively, bending gracefully toward the ground once more. "For you have a habit of disturbing the peace of all who surround you."

I look at him sharply, but his eyes are closed. And I wonder how Sulaiman can claim to know Lela so well.

Frustrated, I head out of the kitchen, back toward the front counter.

When Mr. Dymovsky returns, a box of tomatoes balanced on one hip, plastic bags of produce hooked through his sausage-shaped fingers, Sulaiman and I are barely holding off the lunchtime rush.

"But where is Cecilia?" Mr. Dymovsky cries in his heavily accented English into my ear as he spies his customers' unhappy faces. "Reggie?"

Between orders for sandwiches toasted, untoasted, crusts cut off, cut into triangles, cut into rectangles, with tomato, without lettuce, on rye bread, on white bread—hold the butter, on whole wheat with extra mayo—no cheese, I fill the portly Russian in on what went down this morning.

"The police?" he asks anxiously. "They were called?"

I shake my head. It never even occurred to me to do it, because involving the police would just slow things down for me. "Cecilia, Reggie, and Ranald couldn't leave fast enough," I reply. "And Sulaiman hasn't had time to scratch himself, let alone reach for the phone."

Dmitri takes over the till, wrapping the sandwich orders and dishing them out faster than I can make them. "I shall ask Sulaiman," he mutters in disbelief. "Sulaiman, he is always straight-talking."

During a lull, he intercepts Sulaiman heading out of the kitchen with another tray of warmed-up lasagna.

"Can this be true?" Mr. Dymovsky asks, looking up into the taller man's face. "There was a gun? Shooting?"

"It is true," Sulaiman answers, pointing at the ceiling where a little tag of plaster can be seen hanging down. "You see, there is the bullet hole, sir." He says the words calmly, as if relaying the weather.

Dmitri Dymovsky did not make his tenacious way in a new world by relying on the word of others. While I deal with the tail end of the lunchtime crowd on my own, turning out a succession of coffees that are possibly the worst in recorded history—too cold, too hot, not enough froth, too strong, too weak—the Russian climbs a ladder and picks at the ceiling with a steak knife. When he comes down, he's holding the knife in one hand and the bullet in the other, its cone crumpled from impact with a ceiling beam. His expression is a little shaken.

"Is okay, okay," he mutters finally. "Is tough part of town. So Franklin has gun, who cares? Plenty people have gun, everybody has bad history. We no need extra trouble. Call cops, and Reggie even more angry, Cecilia more frightened . . .

"We shall close early today," Dmitri finishes, patting Sulaiman absently on the back as the cook passes us with another tray of hot fried snacks that will grow sodden and unappealing inside the display cabinet. "You are both good and hardworking children."

At two thirty, when there's no one left in the café except us three, Mr. Dymovsky locks the front door and hands me a mop. He wipes down the flat surfaces and puts all of the chairs upside down on the tables. Sulaiman, paying neither of us any mind, cleans up in the kitchen at his own stately pace, the faint sound of Arabic music weaving its way out of the radio.

Someone pushes the plastic curtain aside and taps on the glass door just after three o'clock. Mr. Dymovsky squints at the dark figure and mutters something that sounds to my ears like *"Likha beda nachalo!"* but I have no idea what that means.

When the person continues tapping and pointing, he shouts, "We're closed! *Closed!* Crazy Aussies, read the sign, why doncha?"

I move closer with my mop and realize that it's Justine Hennessy.

"It's all right, Mr. Dymovsky," I say as the old man makes shooing motions with his plump hands, his gold pinkie ring catching the light. "I know her, she gets her coffee here. I think she wants to speak to me."

He throws his hands in the air and shouts, "What you like!" and moves away with his sponge and spray bottle of cleaning fluid.

I let Justine in and close the door behind her.

"You're finishing up early today," she says in surprise, peering over my shoulder at the abandoned coffee machine. "I was hoping for an afternoon pick-me-up."

"It wouldn't be much of one," I laugh. "Because I'd be making it for you. So it's lucky the machine's been turned off."

"Cecilia's not here?" Justine looks around.

I shake my head. "Neither is Reggie."

I tell her that we had a sort of armed holdup earlier, and her face crumples in dismay. "Oh, I'm sorry to hear that," she says, clearly no stranger to random acts of violence. "I hope no one was hurt."

"Not in any way you could actually see," I say. "But we're down on numbers as a consequence. Was there anything else you wanted?"

Justine hitches the strap of her black leather handbag higher on one shoulder. "Not unless it's a winning lottery ticket." She laughs at her little joke.

Today she's wearing a checked linen shirt over the same baggy white maxidress. Her brown eyes sparkle beneath the purple eyeliner and green-and-pink eye shadow, but there's a new bruise on her cheek, just under her right eye. The thick stage makeup can't hide the fact that it's beginning to go green around the edges.

"I'll walk you out," I say, frowning, and I shake the mop in Mr. Dymovsky's direction to indicate that I'm stepping outside for a minute. He throws his hands up in the air in resignation, then resumes wiping down the benchtops.

"You have to stop this," I say. "It will kill you."

"What? Drinking coffee?" she says brightly, deliberately misunderstanding me. "Everything will kill you in the end."

I frown harder, and she says quietly, "It's okay, I can handle it. I know what I'm doing." And she walks away with a wave. She's good at putting up a front.

I walk slowly back inside, troubled. Sulaiman is hanging up his white cook's cap and black apron in a narrow built-in closet behind the serving counter. My mop is nowhere to be seen, neither is Mr. Dymovsky.

"I have completed the cleaning," Sulaiman says as

he shoulders a small nylon backpack. "Mr. Dymovsky has taken the garbage out to the alley. He says you may go, if you wish."

He holds the closet door open for me, and I pick up Lela's bag, paw through it for her bright red patent-leather wallet, which holds a selection of dollars and coins. I realize from a quick scan of the denominations that there's more than enough for me to head to that Internet place Justine told me about.

I shouldn't get ahead of myself—there may be no response from Ryan. Still, there's a feeling in the pit of my stomach that's more than nerves. Maybe it's hope flowering there. I'm beginning to feel like I'm not floundering anymore, but have to keep reminding myself that I'm just keeping to the plan.

Outside the café, Sulaiman pauses.

"Go home to your sick mother," he warns me. "When night falls you must be away from this place. Do not get involved in the world of men. I say this as . . . as your friend."

I parry his comment with a question of my own. "And when night falls, where will *you* be?"

"At evening prayer, where else? I have many things to be grateful for. That I am alive," he reminds me pointedly. "That I am at peace with my place in the world."

I raise one hand to acknowledge his words, but I'm already walking away. Toward the café with the grinning bowl of noodles sporting arms and legs on its front window, toward the bright theater lights and the ceremonial arch in primary colors.

11

When I make a left turn into the Chinatown precinct, I look over my shoulder briefly, but Sulaiman is already gone. Contrary to what he believes of me, I do want to hurry home to Lela's sick mother. She's not long for this earth, as the saying goes, and I don't want her to die alone.

To face Azrael alone.

The thought pops into my head, but the name does not come with a face or form. I worry at the edges of it as I walk down the hill toward the Internet café, then push it out of my mind as I enter the narrow, air-conditioned chamber filled with machines and wiring. Put it down to just another of the weird lacunae in my memory.

I consult the sign on the wall and hand the man behind the bulletproof booth a fiver. He hands me a token and jerks his head at the room full of computers. "It'll warn you when your time's almost up," he says.

There are only two other people here. A sour-smelling gent near the door who glances up at me shiftily before dropping his shoulders and turning back to face his screen; and an Asian kid in the far corner who looks about fifteen but is probably in his twenties.

I head in the kid's direction. He's playing some ultraviolent warfare game that involves a lot of flame-throwing, fancy weaponry, and people dying in agony in extreme close-up. He doesn't look up when I squeeze past him to get to my terminal.

I insert the token and place the cursor in the little bar at the top of the page, then type in the exact string of letters for the social networking site's home page that I saw Ranald input into his laptop. A few seconds later, the computer asks for an e-mail address and password, and I type in the address I saw this morning and the word *misericordia*, smiling to myself as I do.

It takes me a moment to process what I'm seeing: advertisements for weight-loss supplements, wrinkle-removal creams, and free audio books on a try-before-you-buy basis. Stuff I didn't even know I needed, "tailor-made" for me. But as I stare at the page, I realize that I have one friend online at the moment, and he badly wants to chat.

I study the little window that's popped open at the base of my screen, the miniature version of the photo I've already seen. Read the black text printed there: Damn, Mercy, is it you? Really you? Answer me!

I observe with almost detached curiosity that Lela's hands are shaking a little. It must be after midnight where he is. I can't believe we're together again, after a fashion.

I type: Yes. Ask for proof if you like.

Almost instantly, he shoots back: What's my father's name? My mother's?

I reply, grinning: Too easy. Stewart, Louisa. You can do better than that. I could have gotten those out of a phone book.

He sends: What was the song that Carmen's choir had to learn for the interschool concert?

I reply at speed: Part 1 of Mahler's Symphony no. 8 in E-flat major. Although that's probably publicly available information as well. This is hopeless, Ryan. You can't see me, I can't see you. You might be Brenda Sorensen, for all I know, snooping around. Ask me something only you and I would know.

He's silent for a long time, and I wonder if it really is Brenda digging around in Ryan's computer, or whether I've offended him in some way with my baiting, my acidity.

It's funny how he brings that out in me, how we've fallen straight back into our old way of talking to each other. It's like a defense mechanism, I suppose. No one likes to be hurt, especially not someone who's spent nearly the entire course of her life in hiding. Because I've been forced to, because I can't afford to give myself away. I'm almost poised for disappointment. As the seconds tick by, I almost convince myself I'm communicating with an impostor.

But then words appear on my screen, in fits and bursts so that I must read what's written there twice for it to make any kind of sense.

He writes: Do you think it's possible . . . to fall for someone you've never even really . . . seen?

Luc was right. Ryan may prove to be my salvation, in the end. The blaze of joy I feel is so sudden and so fierce that I find myself literally crushing the edges of the tabletop with Lela's fine-boned fingers. Cracks appear in the particle-board surface where her right hand is resting.

I glance over my shoulder at the middle-aged man inside the booth, to see if he's noticed anything out of the ordinary, but he continues reading his Chinese newspaper without looking up. Only the ceiling falling down would grab the attention of the baby-faced gamer beside me.

I'm suddenly so dizzy, so giddy, I can't type straight, and I need to wait until my sight clears, until Lela's crazy heartbeat is roughly back under my control.

He writes: Mercy? Are you still there?

And I reply, still clinging to that necessary veneer of distance: Can you be specific?

Am I flirting? I'm no good at flirting.

You know exactly what I mean. The words race themselves to fill the screen. This is hard enough.

I reply: Humor me. Humor someone who's had everything they've ever known taken away from them.

There's another long pause.

Then the words: What are you?

He adds: You promised me once that you'd answer that question when we got Lauren back. Then you went and disappeared off the face of the earth.

I feel the corners of Lela's mouth quirk upward, and think for a while before typing cautiously: The people who put me here say that the knowledge is in me. But I can't access it. I'm not a ghost, if that's what you're afraid of. I'm very much alive. And I'm not a bad . . . person. Not anymore. There are things I can do that I don't understand. But I have a physical form. Lauren might have told you. I saw myself in Carmen, can see myself in Lela Neill, as I could in the reflections of some of the others. I'm getting stronger. My ability to remember is beginning to regenerate. But I don't know if what I am is worthy of . . . love.

It's a leading statement and, mentally, I kick myself for even mentioning the word. But Ryan continues to sidestep the real reason we've blundered toward each other again, even though we're separated by oceans, by continents, by logic itself.

He types: After you left, Lauren described you to a sketch artist, a guy we know who's a court reporter. I have his drawing taped up in my room, carry a copy of it in my wallet. I know what you look like. Would know what you look like anywhere. Lauren was the one who saw the resemblance. She knows a bit about art and she said you look like the Delphic Sibyl, but your eyes are brown. Now that's how I think of you. Kind of sacred. Magical. Not of this world.

I make a mental note to look up *Delphic Sibyl*, and write back, grinning: She'd better be pretty, this Sibyl character. So what do we do next?

His response is swift: It's Tuesday where you are, Monday here. I'll be there by Friday your time. There are a few things I need to do here first, a few people I need to talk to. I've started studying again, so I'm playing catch-up big-time. There's a lot I've missed out on. Dad says it's thanks to you (well, Carmen!) that this little miracle has come to pass. And I may just do that finally. Pass (LOL).

Lauren sends her love. She's getting better too. Some days are better than others. But she knows that she wouldn't be here without you, and she wants so much to thank you properly. She's not officially back with Rich Coates, although he doesn't let her out of his sight these days. They spend almost all their time together.

The news makes me smile. Hooray for second chances, I think.

He adds: Don't argue. I know you like to argue. I've already booked a ticket. I know where the Green Lantern is—I've looked it up online. I'll get there in the morning. I'm coming straight from the airport. So just wait for me. Try not to go anywhere until I get there. Think you can do that?

Lela's hands are a little unsteady as I write: That question you asked me? I think it's definitely possible. And I'll be right here, waiting.

I frown, remembering, and add: But Lela might not be able to leave right away. Her mother's really sick. I might need to wait. But it won't be long. Days, maybe hours. Just a feeling I get.

Ryan's response is quick and joyous: See you Friday. Friday! It doesn't matter if we have to wait. I haven't stopped thinking about you since you left. I'll wait. I'll wait forever if I have to.

I don't trust myself to reply, just close out of the chat screen with a feeling in my heart like sun on the water. Though that little voice in my head is reminding me all the while just to *stick to the plan*.

12

It's 5:03 p.m. when I let myself into Lela's house on Highfield Street. The place is so quiet that I'm afraid of what I might find. But Georgia is in the front room, packing up her gear, and she smiles when she sees me.

"See you in the morning, God willing," she says as I show her out.

I nod.

There's a lamp turned on in Lela's mother's bedroom, the familiar whir of the humidifier running in the corner, the smell of incense and jasmine oil this evening. Mrs. Neill turns toward the door as I enter, and her gaze is almost luminous, though her eyes are sunken and the yellow of their whites seems more pronounced than ever.

I grab hold of Lela's chair, and as I pull it closer

toward the wasted figure in the bed, I see that there are tears on her face.

"I'm sorry," she whispers, one thin hand grasping at the air. "I know I've turned your life upside down, darling, and you've got every right to be angry, but you've been so good to me, Lel. You've never once raised your voice, or been impatient with me. No child should ever have to see their parent this way. . . ." She taps at something beneath the covers, attached to her body, and there's a flat sound, as if she's hitting hard plastic. "They've made a jigsaw puzzle out of me, Lel." She half laughs, half cries, and I realize that she's trying to reach out for her daughter's hand. My hand. "Only, nothing quite fits together anymore."

She needs something from me, this woman. She needs permission to go. And forgiveness. And the reassurance that Lela will be okay without her. I don't need to touch her to know it. There's something unfinished between mother and daughter. Something unsaid.

I think of all the hurting words that Lela sensibly confined to her journal and never let pass her lips.

Call me a sentimental fool, but I lean forward and place a hand on her sleeve, murmuring, "I love you,

Mum, in case I ever forgot to tell you that. I love you, and you've never been a burden. You've done everything for me, you've been the best mum I could have hoped for, and I honor you for that."

Lela's mother closes her eyes, her mouth curving up in a tremulous smile, though tears leak out slowly from below her eyelids, leaving tracks down her gaunt cheeks. She doesn't bother to wipe them away, so I do, then I place my hand on her forehead, thinking that the gesture might ease her suffering, as it seemed to do once before.

The tension that is always there, like a knot inside, seems to leave Mrs. Neill's body, to disappear with my touch. Only, it's as if my palm has suddenly become welded to her skin and *I'm* the one with the terminal disease, because, all of a sudden, I can't move.

There's something flowering between us, as if I've opened up a direct connection between my mind and hers, so that if she knew how, she might be able to read *my* thoughts, sift through *my* memories for knowledge of me, the real me, as the *malakh* tried to do.

But no, it's nothing so simple as that.

It's as if something has taken me beyond what's inside the woman's head. I can see inside her body; I have become *of* her body. It's like I've opened a doorway to the grand morphology, the physiology, of Mrs. Neill. Her senses are my senses—I feel the intermittent stab of the morphine pump, the slow release of the corticosteroid in her system, the dull, constant ache of the weeping stoma in her abdomen, the bag that is anchored there. The overheated room, the exterior world, they've disappeared. She is laid out like a map before me: the highways of her bones, the canals of her lymphatic and cardiovascular systems, her connective tissue, her muscles, her nerves. All of them there. All of them laid bare.

Most of all, I feel her great love for her daughter, the howling fear she carries inside, all of it swirling behind that brave facade she buckles on, like armor, every day.

And though every fiber in me rebels, is screaming at me to rise up out of this red-hued world of nightmare, the cathedral of pain, remembrance, and regret that is Mrs. Neill's self-devouring body, I tell myself to go under, to let the tide take me—

I can't begin to describe the feeling.

If Mrs. Neill weren't already unconscious from her latest hit of morphine, I'm sure she'd be able to feel my clumsy spirit navigating the chaotic metropolis within her slight frame. It's like the wildest raceway in the universe, the human body, and I'm being pushed along, I've surrendered all volition. I have no control over the physical world, and no idea where I'm headed, how I'm supposed to use this incredible feeling of power, of . . . boundlessness. Capable of passing through the smallest micromolecule, the thinnest cell wall, yet unable to direct that weird sensation of being sentient yet liquid; mercurial, permeating, yet impermeable.

Once, I was able to do this; once. But the manual's gone. If not erased, then altered, written in unreadable code.

Think. The voice inside me is stern. *Think how it was in that dream.*

That fearful, punishing dream where Luc took us straight through an asteroid. Through solid matter.

I need less of Lela and more of me. That's clear.

If it's truly possible to atomize, to scatter one's energies into any shape one might desire, then maybe I can too, even as damaged as I currently am. I glimpsed the possibility of it in my sleep, and this proves it. The ability resides in *me*. But the mechanism—like the meaning of the word *elohim*—is missing from my recall. Not lost, only forgotten.

Luc told me himself once: *The knowledge is in you.* But where?

I've lost all sense of time and place when I finally chance upon the epicenter of Karen Neill's agony. It's some kind of invasive mass that's an angry red-yellow in color, like a nest of plump worms anchored deep in the walls and surrounding muscle of some long, tubular organ in the body that continuously winds back on itself. There's evidence near the ugly, swelling mass of past surgeries, barely healed, that failed to halt the body's instinct for self-annihilation.

All around me, diseased cells are exploding into life. They divide, mutate, evolve, until they are cannibalizing healthy tissue in every direction. When I come into contact with them, I realize that these cells do not grow old and fade, as cells are supposed to do; they have achieved a kind of voracious immortality; would turn on me too, if I were truly flesh.

I feel like I'm drowning; that if I don't soon find a way out, I will never be able to leave. But I also know that what I'm witnessing is both a privilege and a burden, and

I gather myself like floodwater, like a plague of locusts, and surge through that cancerous mass. I flow through every site of disease and infection I come across, willing myself to burn the sickness from Karen Neill's body, to purge her clean.

But I can't. Everything I see, touch, taste, smell, and feel that carries the taint of illness remains tainted after my passing. Finally a small voice says in me: *This one is meant to die. This one cannot be saved. Azrael has already placed his mark on her.*

There is nothing more to be done.

Immediately, as I think these things, there is a sensation of abrupt coalescence and I am flung out of Karen Neill's body, or pulled back—as if by an invisible elastic cord—into Lela.

I come to, to find myself sweating and shaking and thankful I got out of there alive.

Mrs. Neill sleeps on, dreaming of who knows what.

Finally, I sleep too. Spent.

And dream—not of Luc, of his indelible beauty, his serpentine grace; not of Ryan, Luc's mortal double—but of a fine, silver mist that enters the room. So subtly at first that it is already at the level of my ankles and rising slowly when, in my dream, I wake and rise out of the chair beside Mrs. Neill's bed, leaving Lela's sleeping body still in it.

In my dream, I am myself as I once was. Tall, pale, shining. Like a being made of pure fire.

I look for the source of the fog that is building steadily, taking the warmth out of the air. It is not moonlight that leaves a thin pall of silver over everything: over Mrs. Neill's pinched features, over Lela, sleeping, over the teetering possessions in this room, pushed aside to make way for bedpans and washbasins, a wheelchair and a ventilator, the paraphernalia that dogs the terminally ill, making them seem even more earthbound in their final days.

And I see him.

I give a start, feel a cold flash race through me.

He is standing with his back to me before one of the long curtained windows, his glowing hand holding aside the heavy fabric as he looks out on the moon-stained garden, now overgrown with nightshade and bridal creeper. He has long, gleaming silver hair that spills down his back. And when he turns to look at me—his eyes as blue as the daytime sky but which can darken to near night when he is angered, his face youthful and incorruptible—I know him for who he is, and I bow my head to that vision both terrible and wonderful.

"Lord Azrael," I say aloud, his name recalled at once in the beholding.

Mercy, he says inside my mind, for he has no need for speech. *They tell me that it is what you have taken to calling yourself these days.*

His tone is amused. He approaches me slowly, seeming to glide, his feet never quite meeting the surface of the stretched and faded carpet. Azrael does not prefer the snowy-white raiment that I have come to expect of my erstwhile brethren, my tormentors. He wears what he likes, I remember, so long as it's black.

He stops mere inches from me. He does not seek to touch me, nor I him, because few ever recover from Azrael's touch. Even among the *elohim*—for that is what he is, I realize now, one of the High Ones, almost the highest—he is a power unto himself, a force that straddles worlds and states, life and death. He has no need for stratagems, for politics, the taking of sides. He is power incarnate; the possessor of a singular ability bestowed on none other but himself.

And my dreaming self reminds me that he is here for

his own reasons. I know, without knowing how, that he is not one of the Eight come to gloat over me. Though even in my dream, the irony strikes me as cruel. No doubt when I was first reborn in a mortal body—outcast, bereft, confused, utterly alone—I must have cried out for the services of this man, this being more than man.

Why are you here? I say into his mind. *Why now? You are several millennia too late. I no longer need your "help." I might have once, but no longer.*

There is laughter in his reply. *The years have dulled your wits, my friend. I'm not here for you, clearly.* He raises a shimmering hand and points a finger at the fig-ure in the bed. *But I may not take her yet.*

I frown. *I have seen the ruination of her body, Azrael. Only fear and love are keeping her here. She is ready. End her suffering. Take her.*

Perhaps there is something self-serving in my words. For even in my dream, I know that if Karen Neill is gone I will be free to fly the nest with Ryan as soon as he arrives, leaving Lela's old life behind without guilt, with-out a backward glance.

Azrael's eyes are piercing, and I see that he knows what is in my heart.

By and by, he replies. *But she is meant to go with one other. At the very hour, the very minute, the very instant, the two must go together. And so I must wait to reap them both. But not for much longer.*

In the jump cut way of dreams, I suddenly find myself looking up at him from out of Lela's eyes. Like a djinni called back into the bottle, I am shackled once more inside her body. Azrael seems so very tall now, standing between Lela and her mother's sleeping form. As beautiful, bright, and alien as the stars.

He moves so quickly that I am taken by surprise. He bends low, reaching out with his glowing hands, his breath sweet and warm on Lela's features, mine. The instant he cups the contours of Lela's face, I wake, shaken by the gesture, knowing that if it had not been a dream, Lela would already be dead, and I, fled, gone, departed.

In the early morning, when golden light begins to seep in through the heavy drapes, Mrs. Neill wakes with difficulty and murmurs, "I had the strangest dream, Lel. I thought I woke and saw you sleeping there, in your usual place, but your skin . . . it was glowing. It wasn't moonlight. It was like there was a light on inside you. It was so . . . beautiful."

"It was a dream, Mum," I reply gently, holding up my free hand to be examined. "It's just ordinary skin, highly susceptible to sunburn, as you know."

And the thousand natural shocks that flesh is heir to, I add silently, the words coming to me, unbidden.

I stand up and stretch. "I'll be home early today. I'll ask Mr. Dymovsky if I can cut my shift short so that we can spend more time together."

"Why, love?" she whispers. "It's good for you to get out of the house. I don't feel any worse than usual. Nothing's going to carry me off today."

Her quiet laugh turns into a fit of coughing that goes on and on.

I bend and give her some water, a kiss, tell her I'll see her soon. Not bothering to advise her that Azrael is waiting. Waiting around for that specific purpose.

13

"What do you mean you need to leave early today?" Mr. Dymovsky cries when I tell him what I've decided. "Reggie, she is the no-show. No phone call. Nothing."

We've just survived the madness of the breakfast run, surfing another giant wave of takeout coffees and toasted bacon-and-egg sandwiches. The café is deserted now, save for me, Cecilia, Sulaiman, and the boss.

"Delayed onset of shock?" I suggest halfheartedly.

Mr. Dymovsky rolls his expressive eyes at me. "You are unshockable," he says, wagging his head of flyaway gray hair. "That's precisely why you were hired."

"My mother's dying," I remind him softly. "It won't be long. I can feel it." He searches Lela's face and, satisfied by what he sees there, replies gravely, "Now *that* is a reason I understand. Of course you may leave early. But only after the lunch rush is over. Sulaiman does not have your way with people."

Sulaiman looks up unsmilingly at the mention of his name, returns his gaze to the passable-looking moussaka he is assembling at the kitchen window.

"And Cecilia," Mr. Dymovsky adds, "she is an artist who must be allowed to work her magic undisturbed."

Cecilia beams at us as she wipes down the coffee machine, taking a small sip of her own restorative brew. "You want one?" she asks in her lilting voice.

Mr. Dymovsky tells her to make him one strong enough to add extra hair to his chest. I decline politely because, with milk, without, with sugar, without, it still tastes like poison to me.

There is a flurry of plastic ribbons, then the front door opens. Warm air from the street mingles with the Siberian conditions in here.

"Ranald!" Mr. Dymovsky cries heartily. "Welcome, welcome! Your usual, my friend?"

Ranald nods happily, gives us all a little wave. He sets his laptop bag down on his customary table, rips open pocket after pocket, and takes out a raft of electronic devices I am incapable of naming.

"He likes that," Mr. Dymovsky says to me under his breath. "That we know him, know his habits. He's very complicated, very peculiar. Smart, you know?" He taps his temple. "But almost like a child in many ways. If you get his order wrong . . ." He lifts his eyes to the ceiling, his shoulders and hands in a *Heaven help you* gesture. "Still, the customer is always right, eh?"

He steps forward, picks up a steel ladle, and fluffs up the fried rice warming in a bin beneath the lights of the hot-food counter; moves on to rearranging the fried snacks in neat family groupings with a pair of tongs, while Cecilia starts grinding a new batch of coffee beans for Ranald.

Ranald sees that I am at loose ends and beckons me over, smiling with such genuine warmth and pleasure when I approach that his usually reserved, slightly formal demeanor is transformed.

"Thanks for setting up my profile," I say. "You really helped me out. I wouldn't have known where to begin."

Which is the honest truth. Sulaiman might believe that computers are somehow within God's contemplation, but I'm not so sure.

"I wish everything was that easy," Ranald says with a grin, picking at the ragged thumbnail on one hand.

"But my reasons were purely selfish. I'm calling in that debt—the dinner date you promised me, remember? Now you can't say no. Or pretend you didn't hear me."

"Dinner?" I repeat, disconcerted. "When?"

I hadn't actually promised him anything concrete, but it seems ungracious to remind him of that now. I'd been on fire to get a message out to Ryan, would probably have promised Ranald the earth, the moon, the stars for his help if I'd had to.

"How about this Friday?" he replies. "Just something easy and casual. There's a place I like that's only a couple of blocks away."

"Uh, sure," I say uncertainly. "Friday sounds okay."

By five o'clock on Friday, if it all goes as planned, Ryan and I will be as far away from here as it's possible to get. I've just got to keep on lying like I mean it, until I can disappear Lela right out of her life.

I refocus on Ranald with difficulty.

"Bring your prettiest dress in," he's saying eagerly, "and we'll head straight out after you get off work. I'll take you home later in my car."

"Sure," I say again, neutrally. "That would be great."

"Yeah, it will be," Ranald says, inserting some kind of square portable device into his machine, his head bent over one of the small rectangular slots in the side.

I glance up as someone comes in from the street. Franklin Murray—in the same business suit, shirt, and tie as yesterday. He doesn't look wild-eyed or edgy today. Just numb.

Cecilia takes one look at him and abandons the coffee she's making for Ranald. She hurries into the kitchen, where I can see her peering through the serving hatch from behind Sulaiman's muscular, black-clad shoulders.

"What are you doing here?" Mr. Dymovsky roars. "I will call the police!" Though I can tell from his body language that trouble is the last thing he wants. He and trouble have a history, and he just wants to put it behind him, forever.

"I came to apologize," Franklin mumbles, eyes downcast, mouth trembling slightly. "And to get a coffee and a chicken salad sandwich. My wife thinks I left early for the office. I've been walking around for hours. I've got nowhere else to go." He looks across at Dmitri imploringly, and two tears actually spill out of his eyes and roll down his cheeks, getting tangled in the ends of his mustache, his beard. "I don't know what to do," he wails. "I don't know what came over me!"

I do, but I don't say a thing, because who'd believe me?

Beside me, Ranald is curiously still, watching the interplay between the two older men.

Mr. Dymovsky is red in the face. "No one shoots up my place and my people and gets away with it!"

But Cecilia, Sulaiman, and I act instinctively, a crazy kind of collective compassion moving us that overrides common sense. It's clear that Franklin's desperate, that he's hit rock bottom, and it's awful to see a man unraveling before your eyes. Cecilia comes out of the kitchen and tentatively begins brewing Franklin a coffee, while I seat him at a table near the door. Sulaiman abandons lunch prep for a moment and brings out a small bowl of freshly shredded iceberg for the man's sandwich, his face expressionless but his eyes watchful.

"You're all mad!" Mr. Dymovsky blusters in a voice that's rapidly losing any real heat. "Get him out!"

"You said yourself," Sulaiman reminds him quietly, *"everybody has bad history.* It's past. Leave it there. He won't do it again."

"How can you be sure?" Dmitri says in a low voice.

"You trust," Sulaiman rumbles, moving back toward the kitchen. "Trust. Because you can do no more."

"Lightly toasted?" I ask Franklin in a neutral voice as I see Sulaiman's tall figure, moving past the open serving hatch.

Franklin doesn't look at me, just stares straight ahead and says softly, "Yes, thank you."

His suit jacket is hanging a little awkwardly, and as I move around the table I spy the grip of the handgun jammed into his inside breast pocket, the same as yesterday. The guy's still a walking situation. But that doesn't mean he shouldn't be treated like a human being. We've all been there. It's just that most of us haven't resorted to firearms.

As I pass Ranald's table, he whispers to me conspiratorially, "Is he still carrying a gun?"

I nod almost imperceptibly, and Ranald murmurs, "Who'd ever have imagined a suit like him would be packing heat?"

I fetch Franklin his sandwich and coffee. "There won't be any charge today," I murmur, placing them down in front of him.

There are tears in his eyes again as he answers with dignity, still not meeting my gaze, "I can pay."

I shrug. "You decide."

Mr. Dymovsky gives an audible snort and heads into his cramped little office off the corridor that leads to the poorly ventilated toilets at the back of the Green Lantern. From the stubborn angle of his head and shoulders, the way he's muttering to himself in Russian, he's still debating whether or not to give the police a heads-up anyway.

Cecilia looks at me uneasily as Franklin openly cries between bites of his sandwich and sips of coffee. He's got his back to us, but we can see his shoulders shaking, hear the small animal noises he makes as he mops at his face with the back of his hairy hand.

Ranald frowns at his computer like an irritable turtle. "People are trying to work here," he growls at Franklin, stabbing at his keyboard.

I can tell he hasn't forgotten Franklin's jibe about him being a low-level functionary.

Franklin doesn't respond. He just keeps sobbing and eating, sobbing and drinking, making these awful wounded noises that he thinks we can't hear.

A few coffee orders blow in and out, looking at him curiously as they go by. When I tidy up some loose newspapers sitting by the front window, I see that Franklin's face is a mess. I slide a paper napkin dispenser across the table at him on my way back to the kitchen. He ignores it.

Mr. Dymovsky comes back, mouth in a stern line. He gestures at me.

"Move him on!" he says fiercely, when I return to the front counter. "No good for business, crying customer. Now his stomach is no longer empty? Tell him to cry somewhere else, okay?"

I walk back toward Franklin's table.

Ranald looks up as I pass him. "It's about time you guys did something." His voice is sulky and he's actually pouting. "I can't work in these conditions."

Standing just behind Franklin's left shoulder, I can see that he's finished his sandwich and there's only a couple swallows of coffee left.

"Franklin?" I say quietly. "I'm going to have to clear the table now, because we're about to get really busy." I hesitate before letting my fingers brush against the back of the man's neck. Just the lightest of touches, and

I doubt he even felt it. But it tells me all I need to know. There was a brief moment where I flamed into contact with the man's soul, and all I felt was an overwhelming emptiness. The *malakh* had pushed him over some line he'd never intended to cross in the first place. The gun is still there, but it's there for Franklin alone. Like a personal challenge or a parachute cord, just in case. What I say next surprises me; is the exact opposite of what I intended. "But you're welcome to finish up your coffee and come again tomorrow. Do you hear me? What you did yesterday—nobody holds it against you."

Behind me, Ranald gives a loud exhalation of disbelief.

I hesitate, then place a hand on one of Franklin's pinstriped shoulders. By his sudden silence, his stillness, I know that I have his full attention.

"Just don't do it again, okay? Mr. Dymovsky doesn't want to have to involve the police. Spare your family that, at least. Just tell them what happened with your job, and maybe you can figure out together what the next course of action should be. I think they'll surprise you. Give them that chance. There's a reason you're a family."

I hear Ranald snort again, and feel irritated. Doesn't the guy possess a modicum of empathy? It's almost as if he wants to push the other man into doing something desperate in a public place.

Franklin doesn't say anything and still doesn't look at me as he scrapes back his chair and rises to his feet. I feel everyone tense up when he shoves his hand inside his jacket and starts searching around in there. I turn my head and look across at Dmitri, at Cecilia, at Sulaiman gazing out through the hatch, and mouth silently, reassuringly: *It's okay, okay.* Franklin holds on to the gun's grip for a long moment, as if debating with himself. But after a minute or two, he lets it go and adjusts the front of his jacket with shaking fingers.

It was a gesture of self-reassurance more than anything else, I realize; a reflex action. Like he was telling himself that he still has options.

Without a backward glance, he pulls open the door and bats his way through the plastic curtain.

"I thought he was going to shoot himself this time, I really did," Ranald says as I let out the pent-up breath I'd been unconsciously holding.

Mr. Dymovsky—who hadn't actually heard me invite Franklin to come back again tomorrow—gives me a thumbs-up from behind the counter, but his face is pale and shaken. Cecilia, standing close to Sulaiman near the kitchen door, looks equally stunned. Sulaiman, as usual, appears as impassive and immovable as stone.

It must be nice, I think, to have a faith so strong that a little scene like this doesn't even cause you to break a sweat.

I don't work that way. Fate is there to be meddled with, in my view. Anything else just makes you an observer in your own life.

"It didn't help, you making those stupid comments from the sideline," I snap at Ranald as I pass him.

He surprises us all when he yells in white-hot fury, "Stupid? Stupid is a dead-end waitressing job in a shit-hole excuse for a coffee shop!"

He jams his laptop and doodads into his computer bag and storms out of the café.

"Touchy," I say.

"He didn't even get his second coffee," Cecilia adds in wonder.

"What did I tell you?" Mr. Dymovsky says to me, shaking his head ruefully.

Sulaiman just turns and heads back into the kitchen.

Right on cue, the lunch rush starts and doesn't wind down until after two thirty.

"Okay if I go now?" I ask Mr. Dymovsky about ten minutes later.

"It's okay, Mr. Dymovsky," Cecilia urges. "Sulaiman say he clean up for Lela today. You should let her get back to her mother."

"Go, go!" Mr. Dymovsky says mock angrily, making a shooing gesture with his big beefy hands.

As I shrug on Lela's backpack, preparing to step out into the heat of the afternoon, Mr. Dymovsky places something in my hands. It's a plastic bag holding a large container of rice, with odds and ends ladled over the top.

"You share this with your mother," he says, already half turning away sheepishly. "You eat, and you come back tomorrow and do what I pay you for, okay?"

I turn at the door and give them a wave, and the three of them wave back, each in their own place, each in their own way, so kind that, for a moment, I look at their faces and think maybe it wouldn't be so bad to be a waitress in a shithole excuse for a café in a gritty-pretty city at the bottom of the world.

But then I remember that Ryan is coming for me in two days.

Two days.

And I know that once we're together, all of this is going to seem like a distant dream, and I won't want to be anywhere except where he is, because I'll be one step closer to *free*.

14

I find myself walking faster as I round the corner beneath that ceremonial arch. The air is so hot it's coming off the pavement in waves and making the plain black cotton shirt and skirt I threw on this morning stick to Lela's skin.

I tell myself that I've got it all under control, that it's cool, that I'm just checking my messages, keeping to the plan. But deep down, I'm praying for Ryan to be there, even if it's just in that disembodied, virtual way that I still can't wrap my old-school head around. So that we might occupy the same space, the same time, touch each other's minds, if only for a brief moment.

Not for the first time, I think how this truly is an age of miracles.

Followed quickly by the realization that I am actually setting Luc's plan into motion. Operation Get Me Outta Here is truly about to begin. The sudden burst of happiness I feel is as hot as the sun on the top of Lela's head.

The same guy is on duty behind the bulletproof glass at the Magic 888 Internet Café, which, as far as I can tell, has nothing to do with coffee at all. Only computers. But that's what I'm here for, so I slide my fiver across the counter and he gives me a token in return, without any sign that he recognizes me from yesterday.

I head to a computer away from three boys in identical dark green school uniforms clustered noisily around one terminal; away from the Chinese lady in her sixties with the tightly permed hair and maroon short-sleeved pantsuit who is watching a live-streaming Hong Kong lifestyle program at her terminal and taking notes.

I log in quickly and click on my *Chat* screen.

Hello, beautiful. It's as if Ryan has been waiting for me, and I can't help a wide smile breaking across Lela's face.

I write: Friday can't come soon enough. There's room at my place if we can't leave right away, but don't go reading anything into it, buddy.

He just sends me back two symbols . . .

;)

. . . which takes me a little while to figure out. But when I do, a kooky grin breaks out across my face.

I ask: Do your parents know? About me?

Ryan replies: No. So you'll have to pretend you've never met them before. But they do know that I've invited the Australian girl I've been writing to online to stay for a while. They're anxious about it, of course. But kind of happy that I'm back to being interested in girls and not getting into trouble with the law.

That makes me smile harder.

I write: How many people know about me—the real me?

The fewer people who know about my having been in Paradise, the better. Especially if Luc is planning on the two of us doing a vanishing act from there. Until Luc arrives, I'll need to lie low. Part of me is more than a little uneasy about treating Ryan's home as a hideout, but I have no other options. I know it's cowardly, but I don't want to think too hard about how I'm going to explain it all to Ryan down the track. I'm just going to live in the moment and pray that his feelings don't get hurt when Luc arrives on the scene.

Today, I tell myself, is all about the silver lining, not the cloud.

As I was hoping, Ryan replies: Your secret's safe. Only me, Lauren, and Jennifer Appleton know about you. That's it.

I sit back, relieved. They're all people I think I can trust. They already know that I'm way freaky, so if I suddenly disappear again, they'll just put it down to that.

I'm about to type something else when Ryan gets in first: You might already have seen this, because it's been in the news, here and overseas. But if you haven't, you should catch the YouTube footage of this guy walking on water. Kid you not. He reminds me a lot of Lauren's description of you. The person who posted the video says that she and her BF were making out in a car by a lake in Scotland and all of sudden they saw a glow on the water and a guy at least seven feet tall, dressed all in white, just gliding across the surface for a couple of minutes before he vanished.

Instantly, I feel a chill.

I type, breathing unevenly: Where? Where do I find it?

A moment later Ryan pastes a URL into the chat screen. Over a million people have already looked at this, and it's only been a couple of days. Anyone you know??

I copy the URL, then open another window and paste it into the bar at the top of the screen. There's only one minute and forty-six seconds of footage, but it's possibly enough to make even the biggest skeptic believe there might be something more to life than just the facts.

The man drifting across the surface of the loch is tall, pale, powerfully built, like something out of a classical painting. He has brown eyes and straight, dark brown hair, worn a little too long for fashion; and a strong face that is all angles and planes, with a straight nose, lips set in a stern line. White raiment so blinding that its outline is indistinct. Like a living statue, a being of pure fire, youthful in aspect, yet ageless. A flame is cupped in one hand. By its light, his eyes are searching the depths of that dark water, looking for something. Or someone.

The camera work is understandably unsteady, but

I could swear it's Uriel. So much like me in looks, if not in personality. We last came face-to-face when I was Carmen and he refused to help me find Lauren, or to set me free. One day, I'm going to hold him to account for that.

I watch the footage one more time to be sure, then flick back to the other window, the portal behind which Ryan waits patiently.

I don't know what to say, and hesitate over the keyboard.

Ryan types: Mercy? Did you see it?

Galvanized into motion, I type back: Yes, turns out he IS someone I know. But I couldn't tell you what he was doing.

This time it's Ryan's turn to be silent—for so long that I think he's left the room, fallen asleep, given up on me.

He writes finally: Should I be scared?

My reply is fast: Of me?

He replies: Yeah.

One word. How do I read that?

I type: No, never of me. I would never hurt you.

Then I think about Luc's plan and close my eyes

briefly before adding: But there's some weird stuff
going on with the crowd I used to run with, and
I can't promise that you won't see things that'll
turn your hair white overnight. What you saw on
that clip is just a tasting plate of what these
guys can do. There's a game of tug-of-war going
on right now, and I think that maybe I'm the
rope. You still want to come get me? Don't feel
obliged.

Please, I think. Please still want to come and get
me. I'm almost terrified—me, the person who claims to
rarely feel fear—as I wait for his response.

At last, he types: Yes, I AM still coming to
get you, don't even question that. You and I
aren't done. Flight arrives Friday morning. I'll
come directly to the Green Lantern as soon as I
clear customs. Pack whatever you think you'll
need because we'll go as soon as you say we can.
Stay safe till then. I mean it, Mercy. Stay safe.

I close the window, leave the Internet café, walk
slowly up the hill through Chinatown, the muggy heat
weighing down on me now, where before I welcomed
the warmth.

That footage Ryan directed me to is on constant replay behind my eyes. It's further evidence that two worlds—one seen, one unseen—are beginning to bleed into each other. And I—a citizen of neither, a denizen of nowhere—am doomed to watch from the sidelines and wonder at it.

I stare out the window the whole bus ride home, but don't see anything except Uriel walking on water before vanishing. *What had he been searching for?*

Mrs. Neill is happy to see me, love and relief blazing out of her eyes when she beholds her daughter's face. But she's noticeably weaker today, and as I draw the heavy chair close to her bedside, I can almost see the silver mist rising in the room, Azrael's form standing by the heavy curtains at the window.

I never sleep very well anyway, but that night I do not sleep at all. I just keep vigil, somber and dry-eyed, over the slowly emptying shell that is Lela's mother.

15

Mrs. Neill is still sleeping when I leave to catch the 7:08 bus. I decide not to wake her, because Georgia is due to arrive any moment. I'll ask Mr. Dymovsky if I can have a half day again so that I can be there for her. He has to say yes. Under his no-nonsense exterior, I sense that he's like a marshmallow. Still, he'll be incandescent with rage when I tell him on Friday that I'm quitting. But once he calms down, sees Ryan and me together, he'll understand.

On the ride in, I drink in the sky, the clear, hard light of it, its boundlessness. I'll miss it. There's no sky like this where Ryan lives, in Paradise, as funny as that sounds. It's an ugly place with polluted beaches surrounded by oil-refining and military interests; razor wire; gray from shore to distant horizon.

When I get into the coffee shop, Reggie is back and already angry, although it's only 7:38.

She holds up a hand to me as if she's stopping traffic. "I don't want to talk about it," she snaps.

"I wasn't planning to ask you anything," I say mildly.

"Just get to work." Eyes hard, she jerks her head at the line already forming for the breakfast special: one dollar to upsize the coffee.

Cecilia lifts her eyebrows in welcome, and Mr. Dymovsky smiles at me through the serving hatch, where he's consulting with Sulaiman on the day's menu. Sulaiman acknowledges me with a small nod, and I almost smile. From him, that's tantamount to friendly.

I belt on a clean black apron over my black clothes and get to work with the sandwich press, the sandwich cutter, and long bread knife, wielding them awkwardly as Sulaiman slings out trays of fried eggs and rashers of bacon faster than I can jam them between slices of buttered bread.

As if he brings the lull with him, Ranald's entry into the café signals our first collective breather for several hours. Reggie goes out for yet another "ciggie break."

Ranald comes up to the counter where I'm standing

and says gruffly, "I didn't mean what I said yesterday. About you being stupid. You're not stupid. I wouldn't have asked you out if I thought that. Are we still on for Friday?"

He can't quite meet my eyes, looks at a place a few inches to the right of me, his words scrambling over themselves to be uttered. It's not really an apology, but then again I'm not intending to honor that promise about dinner, so I figure we're about even.

"You betcha," I say. "All set."

I look at him curiously. There's something tight and hard in his features that I can't read.

He stands there awkwardly for another long moment—a moment in which I think he is going to bark something else at me—before he moves away to his regular table and slams his laptop bag down on its surface. He unpacks his jumble of add-ons more noisily than usual and throws himself into his work, not bothering to talk to any of us.

Cecilia looks at me when she returns from handing him his first coffee and shakes her head, her eyes seeming to say: *Do not engage.*

Fine by me, I think. Whatever.

I gaze out the window, seeing a muscular guy in a bomber jacket, with a gleaming bald head, go by, built like an American pit bull terrier. He has a hard weight-lifter's body and some kind of complex Celtic tattoo crawling thickly up the back of his neck in black ink. Must have killed him to get it done.

"Do not mess with that one!" Mr. Dymovsky says as he slides a tray of fried schnitzels into the warming area beside me. He curls his fingers into loose fists and pivots them outward at the wrists as if he's breaking something between them, like an imaginary stick. Or a bone.

Ranald raises his head and says sharply, "Cecilia! This coffee isn't strong enough. I'd like a replacement, please, as soon as you can manage it."

He holds the offending mug out without meeting her eyes, as if she is some kind of servant.

Cecilia looks at Mr. Dymovsky as if to say, *What do I do?* He frowns but nods that she's to make him another one, on the house. *"Délat iz múkhi sloná!"* he mutters darkly.

"I can go somewhere else. . . ." Ranald's voice is silky.

"It is no trouble," Mr. Dymovsky replies smoothly

in English, bringing the replacement over himself. "That is all I was saying."

Ranald sticks his face into his laptop screen and goes back to whatever he's doing, reaching for his scalding coffee a moment later and taking a small sip.

"But I make it the same," Cecilia whispers to me, mortified.

Reggie breezes back inside. "Here's trouble!" she exclaims, shutting the door firmly behind her to keep the heat out. She gazes through the front window from the side just near the door, as if she doesn't wish to be seen from the street.

"What do you mean?" Mr. Dymovsky says, crossing to where she's standing.

Cecilia and I, curious, drift forward too. I wrinkle my nose as I get closer: Reggie's overpowering musky perfume now has top notes of nicotine, bleach, and tar.

"Have a look!" Reggie says, jerking her thumb at a point outside the window. "It's that slut who comes in here sometimes—Lela's friend. From the 'club.' She's having another argument with her boyfriend—looks more like a train wreck than usual."

At her words, even Sulaiman leaves what he's doing

and comes over to where we're standing.

The man with the Celtic tattoo and shaved head comes back up the street in his shirtsleeves, dragging a crying Justine by the elbow. She's got his bomber jacket on now over something that looks like a sequined string bikini, and she's wearing a pair of improbably high stilettos with clear crystal soles and heels—porn star shoes.

"Like I said," Reggie adds with relish, "the slut who comes in here sometimes."

"Not her boyfriend for a long time," Sulaiman says in his deep voice, a frown on his face.

He and I look at each other and, almost in the same instant, throw open the door, and spill out onto the street, Mr. Dymovsky and Cecilia behind us.

Justine and her ex are almost past the front of the Green Lantern when I shout, "Hey, Juz! I've been waiting for you for ages. Aren't you coming in?"

Pit Bull swings around, his fat fingers digging into Justine's elbow like a vise while she cries and tries to pull away. She's almost unrecognizable in her spangled bikini, two sizes too small. Her skin is unnaturally pale under the hard summer sun, and there's smeared makeup all down her face. A thin rhinestone headband is jammed down low over her head like a tarnished halo; her thick wavy hair beneath it scraped back into a low and messy chignon. If the getup is supposed to look alluring, it's anything but. And there's a new bruise on her cheek; I can almost make out the shape of the bastard's knuckles.

"Get back inside, you nosy bitch," Pit Bull replies. "This is between me and Juz here. No law against talking, so stay out of it."

He turns and starts dragging her away. Justine pulls back toward us, pleading, "Help me, Lela! Please!"

I need anger to unlock those powers that are my right, so Luc told me in my dream. But where has my anger gone? I have nothing to draw on except sadness. Justine, dressed like something out of a freak show; Mrs. Neill, with the cheater husband and incurable disease; Franklin Murray, bankrupt, self-pitying, suicidal.

I turn and look at Sulaiman helplessly. Without anger, I could sooner stop a hurricane than stop that man dragging Justine away.

Sulaiman meets my eyes for a long moment, seems to come to some kind of decision that is against his better judgment, because the corners of his mouth tighten as he explodes into motion.

Before Pit Bull can even react, Sulaiman has rushed him and grabbed him by the collar of his checked shirt, wrenching Justine out of his grip and pushing her back in our direction. He shoves the man, and Pit Bull goes down hard onto the hot stinking pavement like a flailing windmill, an audible rush of air leaving his lungs.

Tears streaming down her face, Justine stumbles toward me in her crippling heels, her arms outstretched. I pull her into our tight little group by the door. Mr. Dymovsky moves in front of her, while Cecilia shifts so that she's got Justine's back, the three of us hemming her in so her ex would have to fight his way through us to get to her.

"I'll kill you!" he howls, struggling to push himself up from under the large heavy shoe Sulaiman has placed on his back. "Then I'll kill her! Shoulda done that months ago, the whore."

Sulaiman bends down and turns the man over roughly, his big fists bunched in front of the guy's shirt so they are eye to eye. People on the sidewalk give them a wide berth.

I hear Sulaiman rumble, "She does not consent to go with you, and so she shall not go."

Sulaiman turns to look at us clustered tensely together beneath the front awning of the Green Lantern.

Mr. Dymovsky takes one look at his expression and nudges us toward the front door like an anxious mother hen. "What have we done?" he mutters to himself. "*Likha beda nachalo!*"

I try to get a look at what Sulaiman is doing over Mr. Dymovsky's shoulder, but Mr. Dymovsky waves at me and Cecilia to create a gap in the plastic curtain and open the door. He leads Justine inside gently, hand beneath her elbow, as if she were a small lost child; then I hear him barking orders at Reggie, whose red-painted mouth is opening and closing like a fish's.

As I look back over the counter that runs across the front window, Sulaiman is removing one hand from Pit Bull's face and letting him up off the ground at last. Justine's tormentor stands unsteadily before lurching away up the street, staggering as if he has been mortally wounded, though there appears to be no blood, no wound, on him.

As Sulaiman walks unhurriedly toward the door,

Mr. Dymovsky mutters again, *"Likha beda nachalo!"* Then, "Somebody watch her while I get the first-aid box, okay?"

He disappears down the narrow corridor in the direction of his office, leaving Justine slumped in a chair, her face in her hands, shoulders still shaking.

Sulaiman enters the café, going straight back to his usual station in the cramped galley kitchen as if nothing has happened. Cecilia and I peer up the street together. There's no sign of Justine's attacker. I wonder uneasily what Sulaiman did to make the guy look the way he did as he left.

"Why does Mr. Dymovsky say that?" I ask Cecilia. "What does it mean?"

She shoots me a troubled glance. "It mean 'disaster follow trouble,' something like that. When he worried, he say it. I'm scared, Lela."

"You should be," Ranald says unexpectedly as I close the door.

He says it again, a weird light in his eyes. "You should be."

16

Ranald is long gone, the lunchtime crowd dispersed, when Justine finally stops crying.

Franklin Murray had been among them for a time, sitting on a bar stool at the front window, barely touching his chicken salad sandwich and coffee, reading every single word of the newspaper as if his continuing existence depended on it. When I leaned across him to pick up his plate and crumpled paper napkin, I felt the weight of the pistol in his inner breast pocket brush against my arm. He gave me a frightened look, but I pretended I didn't notice a thing as I sailed away with his plate.

Justine's a tough cookie. She outfaced all the starers that came and went. "Have a good look!" she snapped at some of the worst offenders. "Go on, knock yourselves out."

Cecilia and I try to clean up her face as much as possible with what we have in the shop. But nothing can be done about the new bruise. If anything, it seems to be spreading. Soap and water isn't enough to budge all the eye makeup, and Reggie refuses to lend some remover out of her own handbag.

"Not my problem," she says, her mouth pursed primly like a cat's butt as she stirs the sweet-and-sour pork with unnecessary force. "Don't look at me."

"Like you're some kind of saint," Justine mutters.

"At least I don't get my tits out for strangers *for money*," Reggie replies.

"Sanctimonious bitch."

Mr. Dymovsky shakes his head as the two women continue to take verbal potshots at each other across the room. It's bad for business.

"Take Justine into the office," he tells me. "Then go buy her some shoes, something to wear. It is not safe that she walks around dressed like, like . . ." He waves one hand toward her, looking gallantly at a fixed point above her head.

He gives me a fifty out of the till to back up his request, and I head around the corner to Chinatown, where I go into the first variety store I come across and pick up a pair of men's black kung fu shoes in a size small and Chinese-style pajamas, with change to spare. It's not high fashion, but Justine's still got that creep's bomber jacket, and the ensemble will do until she can get home and into a change of clothes.

She's self-conscious as she slips into the lemon-colored faux silk pajamas in Mr. Dymovsky's office. "Don't look at me," she mutters, changing hurriedly while I stand guard at the door. "I've broken out across my shoulders from all the latex they've been making me wear lately—it's disgusting."

She slips the soft flat shoes onto her large wide feet. They're only a little too big. The bomber jacket she asks me to hand to Sulaiman, and have him throw it straight into one of the Dumpsters outside.

"It smells like him," she says, and shudders. "Don't want it."

Mr. Dymovsky gives me a long-suffering roll of his eyes when the two of us come out of his office. "Of course you can go early, Lela; I was expecting it. And you take care, Justine. Don't go back to that place; you come work here instead, okay?"

"I'll think about it," Justine says, suddenly shy, as we take our leave.

She raises a hand gratefully to Sulaiman. He gives her an unsmiling nod, gets right back to the pizza he's making for tomorrow.

"I think I'm in love with that guy." She laughs in quiet despair as we bat our way out of the plastic curtain. "I always pick the tricky ones—guys on drugs, guys with rap sheets longer than my arm, women-hating latent homosexuals, and now a big Muslim bloke who probably thinks I'm trouble. I'm hopeless. Might as well shoot me now."

I take the sleeve of her Chinese pajama jacket between my fingers and steer her up the road toward the bus stop.

"He's all right, Sulaiman. Not seeing anyone, Cecilia says. Doesn't talk much about himself, bit of a mystery fella. But he's contemplative, spiritual, respectful, no woman-hater, I can vouch for that. You'd have to wear a few more clothes, though, change your line of work, if you've set your heart on him." I grin at her.

She looks down as we cross the street. "Stripping's a crap living," she says sadly. "But it's a living."

"But it's not a life," I say pointedly.

Her reply is weary. "But I'm no good for anything

else, am I? I mean, look at me. I'm a joke."

After fifteen long minutes of Justine tapping on her crooked teeth with her baby-pink fake nails, of Justine itching at her shoulder blades, shuffling her too-big slippers, no bus comes, so we flag down a cab.

When it pulls up, Justine clutches at my sleeve. "Would you come with me? I don't want to go in by myself. He might be there. And you must live close by, seeing as we get the same bus. It won't take long. . . ."

I can feel her tension as she waits for my answer.

I check Lela's watch and see that Georgia will still be with Mrs. Neill for a few hours yet. Bernadette might be there, too.

"Sure," I reply, making another decision almost in the same instant. "And you're welcome to stay at our place tonight. Just in case, you know. We have plenty of bedrooms."

Bedrooms filled with dried flower arrangements, foot massagers, and doilies, overflowing with books and papers, cushions, clothing, hat racks draped in more clothing, plastic bags, shoe boxes, walking canes, and filing cabinets. Rooms and rooms of stuff that soon no one will want.

"I can't promise it'll be tidy, though," I caution. "You'll have to dig yourself out a place to sleep."

"Best offer I've had in years," Justine says.

She gives the driver her address, then falls silent and stares out the window for the entire ride. The cab is filled with pulsing bhangra music and the smell of well-worn leather and stale sweat. When we get to Bright Meadows, I hand over forty-five dollars, waving away Justine's embarassed thanks.

"All my stuff's still at the club," she says.

She gets out with as much grace and dignity as a person with smeared makeup in Oriental pajamas can manage. The middle-aged cabbie gives her a hard sideways look as she slides out the door, keeps looking at her as he executes a slow U-turn and heads back the way he came.

We're standing in front of a 1970s mission-brown brick apartment block with crumbling balconies in a contrasting light beige. Justine can tell from the appalled expression on my face that it's no kind of place to call home. She buzzes someone's doorbell and they let her into the building. The stairwell smells of cooked cabbage and inadequately aired clothing; cats' piss, lost opportunities, a failure to capitalize.

"Got a credit card?" she says when we get to her apartment door.

I'm not sure; hand her Lela's red wallet to rifle through. A second later she takes out a thin plastic card and plays around with the lock. About two minutes later, the door swings wide open.

"There's a reason it's cheap," she says. "Can never lock yourself out. One of the benefits. Wait here for me."

I do as she says, noticing that the narrow hallway is unrelieved speckled concrete. There's rising damp along the baseboards, the florid 1970s wallpaper bubbling up in places as if fed by a subterranean stream. The ceilings are low and there's a pervasive smell of mold or bacteria.

I shudder and move into the external corridor. Oh, Justine, I can't help thinking.

When she comes back with a duffel bag filled with clothes and personal belongings, she locks the door with a spare key she keeps inside, and says brightly, "Lead the way."

A block and a half later and I'm unlocking the door to Lela's house.

"Mum?" I call out softly.

Georgia rises, gathering her things as I enter Mrs. Neill's bedroom with Justine in tow. She nods at Justine, not batting an eyelid at her weird outfit.

There's an awkward expression on Justine's face as she looks around the room. "Lela," she says quietly. "I had no idea."

"She's sleeping now," Georgia whispers, "but she's been asking for you. I'll be here at the usual time tomorrow, but call the number on the fridge if she gets worse overnight. One of the team will respond. She might . . . Not that I trust myself, but it's just a feeling I get."

I nod, my face grim. "Me too. And thanks."

Justine perches in the chair I usually use, so I clear a footstool for myself.

"That you, Lel?" Mrs. Neill murmurs without opening her eyes when I draw the stool closer to the edge of the bed.

"Yes, Mum," I reply quietly. "And I've asked a friend to stay. Her name's Justine."

Justine leans forward. "I won't be any trouble, Mrs.—"

"Neill," I interrupt quickly at Justine's stricken look. We *are* practically strangers.

"Mrs. Neill," Justine repeats awkwardly.

Lela's mum opens her eyes, turns her head slowly, and gives us an unfocused smile. "So lovely to meet you. Lela used to have friends over all the time. It's been months since she's done that."

She swallows painfully, closes her eyes, polite to the finish. "Please make yourself at home," she adds, her voice like something carried on the wind from the afterlife.

She slips immediately into an uneasy sleep, as if the effort of speaking is too great to sustain. I must bend low to perceive that she is still breathing, still with us.

I stand, and Justine immediately stands, too.

"Kitchen's here," I say as we approach the entrance to it. "We can offer you . . ."

I open the refrigerator and see a solitary jar of apricot jam; look in the freezer, see half a loaf of bread— origin unknown, age unknown—and boxes and boxes of a frozen brown pureed substance. Food for Lela's mum, I figure, and I'm loath to serve it, because I don't know what it is.

". . . jam sandwiches for dinner," I finish apologetically.

I'm not often hungry myself, only eating or drinking mechanically when the body I inhabit feels hunger or thirst. It never occurred to me that I might need to actually go shopping for food.

"Jam sandwiches are fine." Justine laughs, a genuine sound of delight. "I like jam sandwiches."

We leave the kitchen, go down the corridor toward Lela's bedroom. "Let me show you where you're going to sleep," I say.

"It's a beautiful house," Justine says as she pads after me in her Chinese pajamas.

I raise my eyebrows at her.

"It would be lovely with just a small tidying," she demurs, something like longing in her tone.

I clear a space on Lela's desk for Justine's bag and tell her to make herself comfortable. I go out to the linen closet in the hall and bring in some new bedding, changing the bed efficiently while Justine looks around the room, runs her fingers along the old fireplace built into the wall, pulls back the curtains to look upon the neglected garden.

"It's lovely underneath," she whispers. "Just needs someone to give it a bit of attention."

And that brings me an idea that I file away for later.

I tell Justine to help herself to whatever she needs, point the way to the bathroom with its 1950s fittings and 1950s concept of water pressure, and retire to Mrs. Neill's bedroom, to my usual seat.

I stay there late into the night while, before me, Mrs. Neill slowly ebbs away.

Or maybe I imagine it, because I open my eyes and it's morning.

Friday morning.

Ryan arrives in just a few hours, I think, suddenly wide awake, every nerve ending thrumming.

I say softly, "Mum?"

Mrs. Neill doesn't respond, and I touch one hand to the side of her face and realize that she's gone beyond hearing, beyond speech. Her weightless soul has already begun cleaving away from the flesh. I know with certainty that there is only a little time left before Azrael returns to complete the division of soul from body.

The first thing I do is call the palliative care team and tell them to send someone over.

"I think it might be today," I say.

"I'll send Zoe right away," the woman tells me kindly. She does not question the certainty in my voice. "Georgia will take over at her usual time. If she's needed."

Though it's only 5:35 in the morning, Justine is already awake and agrees to stay with Mrs. Neill while I head out to the Green Lantern.

"There's just something I need to do at work. I'll be back around midday and you can head off," I say.

"I'm in no hurry," she tells me. Wrapped tight in a woolly robe she's brought from her damp apartment, cartoon-character slippers on her feet, she looks younger, softer, a world away from the teary, edgy woman I accompanied home in the taxi. "I was planning to give notice at that dive anyway. I'll just need to call in at some stage and pick up my share of the tips for yesterday and the pay they owe me. So I'll be officially unemployed as of today. Might do what Mr. Dymovsky suggested and get a regular job." She gives a soft laugh. "Might even take up his offer to work at the Green Lantern."

"You mean it?" I say, delighted. I give her a wide smile. "You couldn't suck at it any worse than I do! And you'd soon show Reggie who's boss."

Justine giggles. "I'd be top dog in no time—Reggie's a choir girl compared to the broads I usually work with."

Her smile disappears, and she's probably unaware of how wistful her voice sounds. "Then maybe that Sulaiman guy will have to start taking notice of me, instead of looking away whenever I come near him. . . ."

"He wasn't looking away yesterday," I point out.

She looks down, scuffs at the threadbare hallway rug. "No, he wasn't, was he?"

She heads off to the shower while I prepare her something to eat. The act of making a toasted jam sandwich hardly calms my strange feeling of nerves. Every sense seems heightened this morning; everything seems brighter, more beautiful, as if newly minted just for me. Even the motes of dust that drift through the air in the sun-stained rooms of Lela's house seem lovely, like tiny winged creatures.

I am impatient to get away; almost leap out of my skin when the doorbell rings, signaling Nurse Zoe's arrival.

I hear Justine answer the door, and place the sandwich I've made for her carefully in the center of the kitchen table. I catch myself wiping Lela's palms on the ankle-length black tiered skirt I've chosen for her to wear beneath a whisper-thin, black Empire-waisted, long-sleeved top. Nerves. Since when do I suffer from nerves? But I feel oddly vulnerable today, sure that my skittish inability to settle is showing on Lela's face.

I head through to Mrs. Neill's bedroom, and the nurse walks in wheeling a heavy medical kit. She takes one look at Lela's mum and says in a low voice, "Do you want the dosage . . . adjusted today?"

I place my hand on Mrs. Neill's brow and shake my head. "She's not in any pain," I say, wondering if my own inner turmoil is obvious in Lela's voice. "She's gone beyond pain."

Zoe places Mrs. Neill's wrist gently on the bed. "I think you might be right."

Justine, in an oversized purple T-shirt, peers in through the doorway, her wet hair around her face, oversize slippers still on her feet, munching on the sandwich I made her.

I step away, give her and Zoe a searching look. "Just stay with her, will you? Stay with her until I get back, and I'll be back as soon as I can. I don't want her to be alone. Not for a second."

They nod, and I head down the corridor after one last lingering look at the still figure in the bed. I'm unable to rid myself of the strange sense that it is the last time I will ever see Mrs. Neill. Well, in this life, anyway.

I hear Zoe snap open the lid of her medical kit, and Justine asks shyly, "Do you want me to help you prop her up?" I close the door behind me with a sense of finality, certain that everything is about to change.

17

The bus ride into town seems to take forever.

I sit behind the driver and bid a silent farewell to Bright Meadows, to Green Hill, to the straggly, fragrant trees, to the power lines and auto parts yards, the gambling dens disguised as family-friendly restaurants, the pharmacies, the bakeries, the banks, the gas stations and supermarkets, as if I will never see them again.

When we finally reach the stop across the road from the café, it's as if I am crossing those four lanes of murderous traffic borne by wings.

He's coming today.

He's in the air right now.

He'll be here in a few hours.

Mr. Dymovsky grins at me over the till when I

explode through the plastic curtain, smiling broadly.

"Somebody is in the good mood today!" he cries.

He doesn't comment on the fact that the clock is showing it to be 6:50 a.m. That I'm almost an hour early for work.

Tempus fugit, they say. Time flies. Of all days, let it be true of today, I think, because it hasn't been doing that so far.

I grab an apron and tie it on. Sulaiman suddenly looms up beside me in that silent way he has of moving around. I take the gigantic tray of bacon and fried eggs he's holding and slide it onto the bench. He doesn't head back to the kitchen immediately. Just stands there watching me cut the crusts off a couple of orders, butter slice after slice of bread.

After a minute or so of his silent scrutiny, I stop what I'm doing, turn my head to look him full in the face.

"What?" I say, refusing to let anything bring me down. Today he can be as cutting, as dismissive, as disapproving, as he wants to be. I will meet all of it with a wreath of girlish smiles. "What am I doing wrong?"

A small frown creases the space between his strong dark brows.

"You should go home to your mother," he says, his words uncharacteristically urgent and uneasy. "Now. Right now. Ask Mr. Dymovsky to give you the day off. He will understand. There is no time to be lost."

I feel Lela's brows shoot up in surprise.

"Thanks for your concern, Sulaiman," I reply quickly, unable to comprehend his sudden interest in Lela's private life. "But it's under control. Someone's with Mum, if that's what you're worried about. I intend just to work out the morning shift and head back around noon. I'm waiting for someone." I break into a grin that I can't hold back. "He's meeting me here and then we'll leave together."

Together. Just the thought of Ryan walking through that door, looking for *me*, makes me feel like hugging myself.

It's almost as if Sulaiman can sense my underlying glee, my unalloyed joy, because he frowns harder, harsh lines etching the smooth dark skin on either side of his strong nose and wide mouth.

"I can't be any clearer than this," he snarls, his face a mask of sudden ferocity. "Get out *now*. Go home *now*."

He points one massive arm at the front door, and

something in the gesture triggers a memory in me wholly unrelated to this dowdy, dated coffee shop. Of a tall man with flaming red hair, emerald eyes, more beautiful than the sun, extending a flaming sword in one alabaster hand. A gesture of anger. Of negation. For a second there is a jump cut between past and present, so intense that I feel I could step from one to the other as easily as leaping between stones.

Then the vision of fury and beauty is gone, and I am left looking up into Sulaiman's angry, mortal eyes.

"Leave," he says. "Leave before it is too late, foolish creature."

Cecilia, at the coffee machine behind us, darts a frightened look in our direction. Reggie pretends she's not listening to our raised voices, but I can tell by the tilt of her head as she hands out coffees and bags of food that she's hanging on our every word.

If Mr. Dymovsky were here, he would find some way to defuse the situation, but he is moving around in the kitchen, whistling a folk song I do not recognize.

I pick up the knife again, something hard and spare, something flinty, rising in me. Who is Sulaiman to order me about in this way? If he knew what he was dealing with here, he would not be so imperious, so hasty.

My words come out more forcefully, more spite-fully than I intended. "I know what you must think of me, of Justine, of Reggie, of all the women around you, with our loose ways, our moral fiber that is so weak and wanting in comparison with your impossibly high standards, Sulaiman. But I refuse to be judged by you. I am past anyone's judgment these days. I am done with it."

I brush back a stray lock of Lela's hair with trembling fingers and force myself to speak more calmly. "Now," I say, "I am meeting someone here today and *we will be leaving together.*"

Sulaiman and I glare at each other fiercely, and I refuse to blink, will not back down. For a moment I get the sense that I can see behind his dark eyes and am disoriented by the fleeting sensation that we have met before.

Maybe in a past life, I tell myself. Stranger things have happened—and frequently do.

"You misunderstand me," he breathes after a moment, looking away, backing down, and the sensation of familiarity dissipates. "Forget I spoke."

He turns and pads into the kitchen without another word.

Reggie looks at me as she jostles fried dumplings with a pair of tongs. "He'll call a fatwa down on you if you're not careful," she says. "What did you do to upset him like that? That's more than I've ever heard him say. To *anyone*."

I shrug, past caring about his good opinion of me, or Reggie's. What is it people say in their broad, laconic voices? Ah, that's right. *Like I give a shit.* I think those words sum up the situation. I'm leaving today. There's no need to play nice anymore.

At that moment, the door opens and Ranald enters, paler than usual, his short hair standing on end. He almost trips over the threshold in his haste to get inside, tightening his grip on his computer bag as if it were an extension of his body that required special protection.

And I go cold. I'd forgotten about Ranald altogether, and that stupid dinner date he'd startled out of me at an unguarded moment.

Mr. Dymovsky, back at his usual post behind the till, looks at him, looks at his watch, looks at the clock, which says 7:12 a.m., and I know that he's thinking the same thing the rest of us are.

Ranald is more than three hours early for his first coffee, but already he seems agitated, buzzy, as if he's been pulling all-nighters and is surviving on nerves and caffeine alone.

He sets up his laptop at the table closest to the counter. Today, strangely, he does not bring forth a multitude of doodads. Just the machine itself and a single device: small, gray, flat, the size of my thumb, maybe. It has a cap, but he leaves that on. Turns the device around in his hands a few times, as if he's studying it with fresh eyes, or seeing it for the first time.

He lines up the laptop precisely with the edges of the table, lays the small device beside it, exactly parallel to the side of the machine. Still, he does not remove the cap.

After snapping his fingers imperiously at Reggie, at Cecilia, calling for his usual coffee, he turns the laptop on. I see that the screen behind a gaggle of icons is pitch black. On it is written, in brilliant white, the words DIES IRAE.

And I feel the world tilt for a moment, on its axis, hear a brilliant snatch of music, a requiem for the dead that I cannot name or keep in my memory. Then the music is gone and the world telescopes, narrows, grows flat, becomes less than the sum of its parts again. But those words, they were the words set to that music. The music of genius, of madness, of death. And they mean, literally, the day of wrath.

Some would prefer the more common translation, I suppose, which is: Judgment Day.

Hours crawl by, in which I am called on to make endless ham, cheese, and tomato toasties, a Vegemite-and-cheese sandwich to go, nine bacon-and-egg specials, and to cut up the "cake of the day," which is to say, the cake of yesterday served with a generous side of canned cream. I am also instructed to take out three loads of garbage, help unload the industrial dishwasher twice, scrub the bathrooms—paying special attention to wiping down the sink areas—rearrange the contents of the ancient drinks fridges, and place the day's salad special—tuna pasta studded with olives and cherry tomatoes—into a sea of takeout containers for the women workers in sneakers who come in looking for a lighter lunch option.

Jobs done, and conscious of Ranald's glowering, agitated presence as he pounds away at his laptop, I collar Mr. Dymovsky in his office and ask him quietly if I can leave as soon as my friend arrives to take me home.

"I don't think Mum is going to make it through

the day," I say, and Mr. Dymovsky can tell from my expression—unfeigned and genuinely sorrowful—that I speak the truth.

"But of course you may go!" he exclaims. "Go now, go whenever you wish."

"As soon as he arrives," I repeat. "And I'd appreciate it if you didn't, uh, let Ranald know of my plans? We were supposed to go out for dinner tonight—he talked me into it, and I regretted it instantly—but that's not going to happen now."

Or ever, says evil me.

"I'm taking the coward's way out," I add. "I'm going to slip out of here and hope he doesn't notice. He'll call again for me after five, but I'll be long gone."

It's my fault—anticipation has made me careless. I just hadn't factored Ranald's stupid morning coffee ritual into my plans for today. Maybe part of me had been hoping that Ryan and I would've left already by the time Ranald arrived with his laptop. All I know is that he can't see Ryan and me together. I don't want to deal with the fallout. Not now. Not today. It's kinder, in a way, if Ranald just never sees me again.

Mr. Dymovsky nods understandingly. "He is a strange fish, that one. Stranger than usual today, I think.

We have a saying: *Ne boysya sobaki, shto layet, a bosya toy, shto molchit, da khvostom vilyayet.*" He laughs at the confusion on my face. "It means, 'Watch the quiet ones.' The dogs who are silent and wag their tails, you know?"

"Uh, okay," I say. I've got one more thing to drop into the conversational mix. "After Mum, uh, you know, well, I might need some time off. To reassess things. Sort out our affairs. So don't expect me back right away. . . ."

He frowns at that. "I understand, Lela. I am not the hard-hearted man. But if you could let me know how long? We are always busy, and Reggie—well, she is not the most even-tempered or reliable—"

"Justine could fill in for me," I say quickly. "She said so this morning. If you were serious about what you said to her, that is . . ."

Mr. Dymovsky freezes for a moment at his desk piled high with papers in English and his native, ornate script that I can't understand. "That dancer?" he says incredulously. "She really would like to work in my little coffee shop? I would not have thought . . ."

I nod. "She's a good person, she really is. And she can't keep doing what she does. It will kill her, one way or another."

His face is grim as he recalls the scene outside the café yesterday. "God protect us from such people," he mutters. "God and Sulaiman will keep us safe. I know I was right to hire that man."

I push my point. "And she's aware of the uniform policy around here. Black. No sequins." I grin.

Mr. Dymovsky smiles tiredly. Today he seems more seventy-five than fifty-five as he shuffles documents from place to place with his big hands.

After a while he says, "You tell Justine to come and talk to me, and we shall determine if a coffee shop is where she belongs."

Satisfied that I've put a few things out there that will make it easier for Lela's coworkers to rationalize her sudden disappearance, I am turning away when I remember something.

I ask Mr. Dymovsky for a blank piece of paper. On it I write:

I, Lela Neill, of 19 Highfield Street, Bright Meadows, leave all my worldly possessions, both present and future, to Justine Hennessy, also of Bright Meadows.

I sign it with an indistinct, made-up signature, print Lela's name beneath it, push the paper under Mr. Dymovsky's nose, and ask him to sign it, too. And date it for good measure.

"Put in the time, too," I say. "So there's no uncertainty about when it was written."

Mr. Dymovsky does what I ask without question, but hesitates before he pushes the paper toward me.

"Are you sure you know what you are doing, Lela?" he says, his expression deeply troubled.

I nod and fold the paper. "I'm sane, and I know what I'm doing, Mr. Dymovsky. No one forced me to do this. Remember I said that. It's an insurance policy, of sorts."

For Justine, I think. For Justine.

He shakes his head at me uncomprehendingly.

"It's been a privilege working for you," I add. "Like balm for the soul. You're a good man. Decent. I couldn't have hoped for a better boss. And I wish you . . ."

For a moment I am at a loss for words. The Latin is at my fingertips, but not its English counterpart, and the phrase tumbles out before I can catch myself.

"*Bona fortuna,*" I say. "That is what I wish for you."

Mr. Dymovsky's answering smile is surprised.

"Good chance, good fortune," he replies. "And to you, Lela. But you speak as if we will never meet again, and that is not the case?"

I shake my head quickly and leave his office, not trusting myself to say any more.

18

Ryan, I think, as I stand by the service area surveying the dining room, *where are you?*

I wonder if he looks the same. I wonder if he'll recognize Lela, recognize me. If he'll be able to adjust to the new face and form I'm wearing. I need to get to him before Ranald sees him. He can't see us together.

It's 10:53 and there's no one in here except Cecilia, Reggie, Sulaiman, and Ranald.

Ranald looks up at me sharply when I slide back behind the counter to place the paper into Lela's bag for safekeeping, intending to hand it to Justine at the appropriate moment.

"Do you want to check your messages?" he says curtly. "There's still time."

Without waiting for my reply, he gestures brusquely for me to sit as he gets up and heads to the bathroom. Given that he's on his third double espresso for the morning, it's a wonder neither Ranald's bladder nor his heart have exploded yet.

I slide into the seat, made warm by his body heat, and there's Lela's profile page.

There's a single comment posted on the wall beneath her photo and name.

Lauren can't wait to see you, and neither can I. They're calling me to the plane right now. All that separates us is one day, Mercy. A day. Can you believe it? I'll be there soon.

It was posted yesterday morning, and I think of Ryan taking the time to reach out to me at some anonymous airport computer terminal, and feel almost giddy.

Then there's a flurry of movement outside—as if by thinking it I willed it into being—and the door opens. And Ryan is standing there, a duffel bag in one hand. Wearing that beat-up leather jacket over layered tees, one blue, one gray, indigo jeans, scuffed boots. His dark hair is longer than I remember. I suppose he hasn't cut it since the last time I saw him.

He's still lean, but powerfully built, heartbreakingly beautiful; all the more so because it's not what he's about. There's no vanity in him, just an instinctive athlete's grace. His dark eyes widen further as they fall on me.

He's dressed too warmly for the day, and he's flown for hours just to get to me. His face is so pale with weariness that I move toward him, fingers outstretched, as if the touch of my hand might banish his fatigue. That familiar fringe of black hair falls into his eyes, and I reach up and brush it back as he looks down into Lela's face and says softly, "Well, there you are."

He seems so tall, taller than I remember him, even though Carmen is short and Lela is short and there shouldn't be any difference in perspective at all. But something *is* different this time, because there's no hesitation, no dancing around the truth. He just pulls me to him and murmurs, *"Mercy."*

His arms about me feel so right, as if it's always been this way.

But it's never been this way. It's only ever Luc who's held me like this, whom I've allowed to hold me this way—arms around my waist, linked at the small of my back, chin resting atop my head, warm breath stirring my hair. So close, I can't be sure whose heartbeat I'm hearing, his or mine.

Ryan tightens his hold on me, and I wonder how it is that I never even felt Luc's iron grip over my heart loosen enough to let Ryan in. After all this time, out of all these lives, to find myself falling for someone when it's the last thing I should be doing, when it screams *forbidden*. It's terrifying.

In answer to everything unspoken that I'm feeling in the hard muscles of Ryan's arms, I tentatively place Lela's cheek against Ryan's shoulder and breathe in his achingly familiar, addictive, clean male smell before smiling up at him out of Lela's eyes. And I know it's the wrong response, it's not what I want to do, but I don't know if what we are together is even . . . allowed.

Ryan tips my face up to his, searching my eyes, wanting more. But I reach up with one hand and place a finger to his lips.

He sighs in resignation, kisses it anyway. And I pull my hand back from him so quickly—as if his touch has the power to burn—that he throws back his head and laughs.

He's so tall, I think, dazed. Somehow I imagined us being equals when we met again—in every sense—but this is the real world, and in the real world I look like Lela. There's no getting around it, though I can't help wishing that he could see me the way I really am. I wonder whether he'd approve and like me even more if I was wearing my own face, if we were eye to burning eye.

He swings me around gently, the better to look at me, to see me behind Lela's eyes, to imprint this new face on his consciousness. And I catch a glimpse of Cecilia smiling widely behind her coffee machine, Reggie's open-mouthed, gobsmacked expression, Sulaiman's dark, unwavering gaze through the serving hatch that frames him.

Then I remember.

"There's no time to explain!" I exclaim, suddenly shoving Ryan in the direction of the front door, so hard that he actually stumbles a little. "There's a guy here—he's in the bathroom—and he can't see you. He just can't."

Ryan digs his heels in, stands straighter, looks around. "Who is he? What does he want?"

I shove him with every muscle in my body, but now

it's like pushing an unyielding stone.

"You don't understand," I say, tugging on the duffel bag in Ryan's hand. "I promised I'd go out with him tonight if he helped me find you. I would've promised him the world. He can't see you. You've got to go. *Now.* Just wait on the other side of the road. Outside the tapas bar." I point through the window, through the plane trees in the middle of the road, to a sign with the outline of a black bull on it.

Ryan's face is mutinous, and he tightens his grip on me. "I'll clear it up with him. He'll understand. He'll have to. How could he hold you to that if he sees us together?"

"No time," I say. "No way to let him down gently. It's too complicated to go into now. Just wait for me and I'll come to you. I won't be long. Wait for me?"

Ryan's face clears and he bends and takes my face gently in his hands.

I know what he's trying to do, what's in his heart. I can feel the heat through his skin, an answering heat rising beneath mine, and I freeze, fear and desire at war within me.

He sees the look in my eyes and smiles.

"Only if you want to," he breathes, his eyes hynoptic as he inches closer. It's something so longed for that I slide my arms around him again, amazed at myself, at my temerity, almost succumbing to the moment before pushing him away.

"Not now," I mumble. "I need time to work us out, and that's the one thing we don't have right now. You've got to go."

He sighs. "I can afford to be generous, I suppose." But I can feel his reluctance to let me go even as he's pulling away, out of reach.

"Wait for me," I repeat. And it's not a question.

His smile crinkles up his eyes and makes him seem lit from within. "Until the end of time," he says quietly, and leaves with another flurry of the plastic curtain, waving once at me through the window before crossing the road.

When I turn around, Ranald is standing silently beside the service area. I don't know how long he's been there.

I rush over to his laptop and log out clumsily, saying, "Thanks. All yours again."

He glares at me and I look away, almost bumping

into him in my haste to put some distance between us. There's guilt mixed in with all this, too. I can't bring myself to tell the guy that dinner tonight is out of the question; that it's out of the question forever, because he and Lela will never have a future. Lela is riding into the sunset with someone Ranald can never measure up to. Not in a million lifetimes. And he's standing right across the road at this moment, probably hailing us a cab.

Ranald's eyes blaze into mine for an instant, as if he can read my thoughts. But then he sits down and flicks impatiently between a couple of open windows on his laptop, as if he's waiting for something to come through.

I feel like I've been dismissed, and I am ridiculously relieved. He didn't see. He can't have, the way he's staring so intently at his screen.

The mailman bustles in and leaves a sheaf of mail with me for Mr. Dymovsky. Unable to stop myself, I peer out through the window at Ryan's waiting figure, before taking the mail to Mr. Dymovsky's office. He looks up gratefully, but his thoughts are elsewhere and his thanks are distant.

"The café is still quiet," I say at the door. "And my friend has arrived. I was thinking I might leave now. . . ."

Mr. Dymovsky nods and says in his usual way, "What you like, Lela, what you like," before returning his gaze to the correspondence in front of him.

I'm heading for the cupboard to get my backpack when Franklin Murray steps through the door, meeting my eyes sheepishly. He sits with his back to everyone, near the front of the café, and pulls the day's newspapers toward him with a heavy air.

"Ah, the prodigal bankrupt," Ranald says loudly, with satisfaction, and for a moment his fingers are still on the keyboard of his machine.

Reggie takes one look at Franklin and flounces out of the shop with her cigarettes and lighter, declaring, "It'll be a cold day in Hell before I serve that son of a bitch again!" I know she's still holding a grudge against him and won't be back until he leaves.

There'll be no one to make Franklin's sandwich and serve him coffee if I go right now. So I change direction away from my things and head back to the breadboard to set about organizing Franklin his usual meal while he loses himself in his newspaper, as if the answers to his misfortunes are somehow encoded there.

Just as I'm placing Franklin's coffee down on the

table, Justine bats her way through the greasy plastic curtain into the cool of the shop. She closes the front door firmly behind her, pushes her loose fall of heavy hair off her broad shoulders, and looks around.

"What are you doing here?" I say, wide-eyed. "Is everything all right? Is she . . . ?"

"No!" Justine responds hastily. "She's just the same as when you left. Sorry if I scared you, coming in like this."

She walks over to me, oblivious to the way Franklin stares, sandwich paused halfway to his mouth, the way Ranald's eyes greedily follow her around the room. She's modestly dressed in a denim skirt, sandals, and the same oversized purple T-shirt she had on this morning. Not a scrap of makeup to hide the bruises on her face. But she looks in control today, tough as nuts.

"The nurse said it'd be all right if I ducked out for a couple of hours just to sort out my pay situation and maybe speak to Mr. Dymovsky," she tells me. "See if there's really a job available. It'll mean taking a huge pay cut, but it'll give me a chance to get myself together. The hours are better, too. And there's plenty of muscle on the premises to keep Bruce off my case. . . ."

She glances into the kitchen at Sulaiman's back, and I smile despite the tension I'm feeling.

"Mr. Dymovsky's in his office," I tell her. "I'll show you the way."

And then, I promise myself fiercely, *I'm getting the hell out of here.*

Behind us, I hear Ranald say, "Where's my coffee, Cecilia? What's the holdup?"

He's annoyingly imperious today, but I don't really care, because Ryan's waiting for me, and I will shortly shrug off all the petty irritations of this life as a snake would shed its skin.

19

I leave Justine and Mr. Dymovsky chatting away together like old friends and return to the front counter. It's 11:27. Wherever I am in the café, whatever I'm doing, my eyes keep returning to the window.

Sulaiman turns up the volume on the Arabic station he always has playing. Begins to hum along to some incredibly complex tune that keeps rising and falling. It's beautiful. Otherworldly. Like a muezzin's cry—a call to prayer set to music.

He looks at me through the window between us. "It's too late to leave now." His tone is almost conversational; there's no longer any heat in his words.

I have no idea what he means, and I snap, "But I *am* leaving now," unable to comprehend the man's sudden interest in Lela's comings and goings. "And no one—not you, not anyone—is going to stop me."

Sulaiman shrugs as if he's lost interest in the conversation. "Tell that to him," he says, pointing over my shoulder.

I turn to see Ranald get up from his table and head to the front window, look out into the street. First to the left, then to the right, as if he's about to cross a busy road. I wonder what he's searching for on that congested streetscape, the construction site nearby filling the air with clamorous bursts of noise.

Then his gaze settles on something in the middle distance, and I follow his line of sight, catch Ryan speaking to a passerby, a woman on the street outside that bar. I feel an involuntary smile curve up the corners of Lela's mouth as Ryan throws back his head and laughs at something the woman says before she moves on with a small wave.

Mine for the asking, mine for the taking, I think greedily as Ryan paces the street a while longer before disappearing inside the tapas place.

But then something like melancholy steals over me. Because in no universe could Ryan and I ever work. We were not made to be together. We were not made for each other. That emotion *love* is for humans and . . . well, you know the rest.

As I tear my gaze away and refocus on the dingy dining room, Ranald purposefully closes the front door, turns the lock, and flips the sign over to read *Closed*.

"What's he doing?" I ask Cecilia, indicating Ranald with a jerk of my head.

Cecilia looks at me, puts down the jug she's holding.

Ranald turns and addresses all of us. "You know what it would take to get your attention, to get you all to really *look* at me?"

Franklin doesn't bother doing that, just keeps reading his paper. Ranald shocks us all by grabbing him suddenly by the hair above one ear.

"Hey! Wha—" Franklin cries out as he's pulled out of his seat, away from his paper, his half-drunk coffee, the neat, twinned crusts of his chicken sandwich.

"My life is full of pricks like you," Ranald roars. "Who won't even do me the courtesy of looking me in the face when I'm talking! I said, do you know what it would take to get your attention, you asshole?"

Franklin, his head pressed into the front of Ranald's suit jacket, squeals, "No! What? *What?*"

Ranald shoves his free hand into the front of Franklin's jacket and pulls out the handgun. "Violence," he snarls, shoving Franklin away from him so hard that the older man misses the edge of his seat and falls on the floor. "In point of fact, Franklin, I was lost and you showed me the way. So did that slut and her lowlife boyfriend." He smiles. "A little violence, I've learned, can focus people's attention *enormously*."

He kicks Franklin so hard in one leg that Franklin shrieks in agony.

"Get over to the counter, you fat-cat bastard," he orders. "And put your hands on it where I can see them."

He waves the gun in Sulaiman's direction. "You too, big guy. And you." He points at Cecilia, whose eyes are huge in her terrified little face.

"I'm sorry you had to get caught up in this," he says to her, almost kindly, "but I need you to witness what happens to people who betray and belittle me and insult my intelligence."

"What is this noise?" Mr. Dymovsky snaps, emerging out of the dark little corridor at the back of the shop. Justine is behind him, her eyes wide. "Who insults whom?"

Ranald stops them both in their tracks by leveling

the gun at Mr. Dymovsky's chest. Mr. Dymovsky's resemblance to Humpty Dumpty is more pronounced than ever: his rounded eyes and mouth, his too-tight, slightly shiny pants worn a little too high.

"Do what I say and you won't get hurt," Ranald murmurs silkily, using the gun to wave them both over to the front counter, where the others are clustered, hands outspread. "Only those who have hurt me get hurt today. So be a good sport, Dmitri, and you'll see out the rest of your life comfortably."

Justine gives a muffled whimper as Ranald pushes her into place beside Mr. Dymovsky, Cecilia, and Franklin. He strokes the back of her hand, and her face goes pale and tight, as if she wants to throw up.

"Someone like you wouldn't even look at me unless I was paying, would you?" he says, running the barrel of the gun down the side of Justine's bare arm.

She turns her bruised face away, twists her body, every action a rejection. Ranald raises the gun sharply, as if he's going to hit her with it, and Justine cringes. But he laughs and lowers it again.

"It doesn't matter now," he mutters. "There's only ever been one girl for me, and I'm done with her playing hard to get, with waiting around. Done with being treated like rat shit by everybody in my life, especially by her."

He looks at me with his burning gaze, and I realize whom he's talking about.

"You can't mean *me*," I exclaim.

I recall Lela's journal. It was Andy this and Andy that; Ranald hadn't even entered her headspace. He'd been nothing to her. Nothing. And I'd done nothing to encourage him.

Except, says my inner voice, *agree to have dinner with the guy.*

I move toward him now, more ticked off than afraid.

"You mean you're doing this"—I wave my hand at our surroundings—"because I've hurt your feelings in some way?"

"In some way?" he yells. "*Clementia* would have been a better password than *misericordia*, don't you think? Remember, I speak Latin. You've lied to me from the beginning."

He waves the gun around, and everyone ducks and cries out, except for me. I look at him, stunned, as the meaning of his words begins to sink in.

His tone grows almost conversational. "The conno-tations are so much less negative, I would have thought. Clemency versus the cry of the miserable damned. Why choose the latter and not the former?"

"How did you know?" I say stupidly, and in that instant, I realize. I should have seen it before. I'd been too blinded by making contact with Ryan to take in what else was going on. Ranald had set up Lela's profile page for me, logged in for me on his way to the damn bathroom this morning. He'd known the password I'd selected, had even entered it for me, although it was sup-posed to be something that I'd come up with, for my eyes alone. But what was worse was that I'd never changed the e-mail address Ranald had inputted in the first place. It was *his* e-mail address. I'd been using it ever since; had had no idea that he might be able to monitor my mes-sages, that he'd even *want* to do that.

"I've seen every single exchange between the two of you," Ranald spits. "I'm a software developer, remem-ber? It's my job to think like a hacker, act like a hacker. Even if you hadn't been a stupid bitch and left my e-mail address attached to your account as your point of con-tact *with the entire world*, I would have been able to get in and read everything you wrote. Nothing you could do online is safe from me. You're pathetic, Lela, you really are. Did you get off doing some kind of weird role-play with a stud overseas while you strung me along? Home-grown guys not good enough for you?"

Sulaiman says quietly, as if thinking out loud, "For length of days shall not be theirs."

"Shut up!" Ranald screams, shaking the gun in Sulaiman's direction, cocking the hammer. "Shut up, or I will shut you up permanently, you religious fanatic."

With his free hand, Ranald grabs my shirt and pulls me across to the table that has his laptop on it. Training his gun on me, he lets go before uncapping the little gray device resting on the table and jamming it into a slot on the side of his machine. He flicks open a draft e-mail, then opens the window for the device. There's only one file in it. He attaches it to the e-mail, all with one hand.

"I've spent all morning crafting an emergency anti-virus update e-mail for P/2/P and its entire list of clients," he says. "Each one run by truly incompetent twits who wouldn't know how to spell 'Trojan' let alone recognize one or appreciate the indignities I suffer—the bullying, the finger-pointing, the backstabbing—to keep the reams of crap they generate safe from people like me. Press *Send*, Lela. Their networks all across the country are going to *implode*, and you're going to set it in motion. From here. From the Green Lantern. I said I'd take P/2/P down with me one day, and now everyone's finally going to believe it."

His laughter sounds like despair to my ears.

"What if I say no?" I reply. "The police are outside. A whole pile of witnesses."

I point through the window. While Ranald's been busy unleashing his narcissistic inner demon—that small boy who found it amusing to douse his pet mice with gas and set them on fire just to see what would happen—he's failed to notice armed police officers erecting plastic construction barriers across the front of the coffee shop, redirecting traffic. Ranald didn't see fit to draw the blinds when he decided to take hostages in the middle of the city, and now a crowd is beginning to build, because it's human nature to want to stare at the car crash, count the injured and the dead. Ambulance personnel are moving into place on one section of the street, and there are news crews gathering.

"I know they are," Ranald replies tonelessly, hammering the *Send* button on his laptop. "I told them to come."

"That doesn't make any sense," Franklin blusters, but I don't hear Ranald's reply because one face in the crowd has drawn my gaze: ashen and heart-stopping, eyes shadowed from a long-haul flight during which he probably did not sleep. Someone who's six foot five and built like a linebacking angel.

Ryan.

My hands fly up to my mouth, all the fear I feel for him in my eyes. Why didn't he stay inside that bar? What if Ranald sees him?

When Ryan's eyes meet mine over the heads of the people in front of him, something flares in them and he pushes his way forward until he is standing right up against one of the plastic crash barriers. The width of the sidewalk away.

I shake my head, mouth at him to *go away*, but he stands his ground stubbornly.

"What's happening?" he shouts at me through the glass.

I shake my head again, my face telling him that it's too hard to explain, my eyes telling him to run.

The harsh midday sunlight is reflecting off the surface of the windows. Ryan probably can't see Ranald standing behind me with a gun leveled at my back.

I see Ryan turn and collar a policewoman who's standing nearby. He points in my direction. She squints at me through the glass, shakes her head.

"You can't go in there, sir," she says. I hear her clearly, though she's standing outside.

"That's my girlfriend," Ryan yells. "My girlfriend in there. I need to get inside."

And without thinking, I walk away from Ranald, the psychopath holding the gun, toward the window. I touch my hand up against the pane, my heart so full I almost can't contain it.

Ryan smiles at me, but there's a terrible fear in his eyes as Ranald approaches quickly and wraps one arm around my neck from behind, the other hand still holding Franklin's gun, his breath foul with coffee, sleeplessness, adrenaline.

I'm rarely afraid. And I have no sixth sense, no ability to foretell the future. But everything about this bright morning—this morning in which everything seemed more beautiful than it was possible to be—is going badly wrong. It wasn't supposed to be this way when Ryan and I found each other. It was only meant to be the first step. Today was supposed to be all about the silver lining, not the cloud.

"Give yourself up, sir!" a policeman shouts at Ranald through a loudspeaker. "All the entries and exits are blocked off. There's nowhere to go. Give yourself up quietly or we're coming in."

I wonder how someone who looks like Ranald on the outside—composed, professional, pleasant—can hold so much vitriol, store so much rage and envy inside. How he could blame Lela Neill for tipping him over the edge when all his life he's been poised to fall; poised to explode like a Catherine wheel, raining fire down on everyone.

"You've done what you came to do," I say. "Sent out your hydra made of code and malice, your virus strong enough to bring down entire companies. Let everyone here go. Let *me* go. You may not wish to live your life, but I do. I've traveled so far to get to this point. A long time ago, I was standing in the place you now occupy, and I was not destroyed. I chose life, or had it chosen for me, and I have stuck with it. It may not be the life I would have wanted for myself, and yet I embrace my future. And it is out *there*."

I point at Ryan through the window, feel the surge of that sea I carry inside me. I meet his gaze; his heart in his eyes, too.

"Let me go," I repeat. "Please."

Ranald clutches me more tightly to him, sticks the point of the gun into the hollow between Lela's collar-bones for effect; to see the devastation it wreaks on Ryan's face.

"You were never going to go out with me tonight, were you?" he says calmly.

I shake my head, and the cold muzzle follows my every movement as if it has become one with me.

"I'm sorry," I say, "but we would never have worked, not in any life."

When he continues to hold me, saying nothing, I can't stop myself from remarking peevishly, "You'll never get out of here alive, you know."

"I know," he whispers, placing a kiss on Lela's head.

I see Ryan blanch; feel Lela do the same.

Ranald pulls me in closer, pushes the muzzle harder into the base of Lela's throat. "And neither will you."

Then he shoots me. *Us.*

The crowd outside shrieks with one voice. No doubt leans forward, all the better to see.

I feel myself fall backward to the floor, numb with shock. Fall upon his body, already dead. His soul already departed; Azrael not here to reap it.

Blood, like a fine rain, a gentle mist, seems to fall upon us, and I hear Ryan screaming through the glass, "No! Mercy, *no!*"

20

Ranald shot Lela up through the hollow of her neck, a shot that exited her body and went through his heart. He did that deliberately, wanting a quick death for himself, but for Lela to die in terror and pain, air and blood mingling in the cavity he'd made in her body. He wanted her to be entirely conscious as her life ebbed away.

Except that *I*, not Lela, am the one bearing witness. I can feel her inside, locked away tightly, like a kernel, a hard knot, within her own body, her soul twisted, turned in on itself, like a Möbius strip. It's highly likely she feels nothing, sees nothing, doesn't even realize that she's dying. And that, itself, is a mercy.

The pain I'm feeling from the gunshot wound is visceral and immediate but tolerable. Easily subsumed by someone with my strange . . . abilities. But Lela's spinal cord has been severed, her lifeblood is leaching out and mingling with Ranald's on the floor. Even as I try to coalesce inside her, push all of myself into those ruptured, crushed, cauterized areas of skin, bone, nerve, and muscle in order to knit them together, in order to staunch the bleeding, purge the wounds of cordite, make her rise, make her walk again, make her whole, I know that she is failing. That I have failed. That I cannot heal Lela, as I could not heal her mother. For a moment, I imagine that Ryan is here beside me, holding my hand. But it must be an illusion thrown up by Lela's dying mind, for I hear Ryan outside screaming, "Christ, please! Let me go to her, *please!*"

There are footsteps all around me, but the world is growing dark and I am more entombed, more earth-bound, than I have ever been, for the body I am shackled to is growing cold.

My inner demon, always one beat ahead of my waking self, says: *This one is meant to die. This one cannot be saved. There is nothing more to be done.*

And I recognize that for the truth, want to tell them all—Mr. Dymovsky, Cecilia, Sulaiman, Justine,

Franklin—that there is no point separating Lela from her murderer, no point throwing open the front door, screaming for help. The stretcher, the defibrillator, the tourniquet, all the medical marvels of the age, are wasted on Lela now. But I cannot make my voice work. For her body is dying, and her senses are fading, and I am mired in them.

I should have seen it coming; it had already been foretold by Azrael himself. He had touched the side of Lela's face, marked her as his own. I'd misread everything—had thought Azrael was to take Mrs. Neill and some stranger. The two to be reaped at the same instant. Not a stranger, I realize now. Lela. Mother *and* daughter.

And I'd dismissed Ranald all along when I should have seen. . . . Because I did see, but did not understand.

"Oh, Lela!" It is Justine, crying tears of salt over Lela's mortal wounds.

Someone cups the side of Lela's face, and I imagine it is Azrael come for us. He picks Lela's body up off the cold linoleum floor, cradling it tenderly against his broad chest. And I feel a warming pain in my extremities, in my left hand, as if it comes not from me but from his touch.

"Mercy," he says into Lela's blind eyes.

But *I* am not blind; *I* am not deaf. I may be trapped within Lela's body, but I know that voice. It is not Azrael after all. But Sulaiman.

I say his name, my lips moving soundlessly, and in the saying realize that I know him. Not just Sulaiman inside, no. Lela's eyes may have failed, but not mine. When he holds me to him, I see him and know him and remember that we were friends once.

He is one of the Eight. And his name is Gabriel.

Some know him as Cebrail, as Jibril, as Gavriel, as Jibrail. He is known by many names, the herald of mysteries, the light and the mirror. He has been hiding the brilliance, the pure energy, of his being within another. All this time, he was here. In plain sight.

He can take any form he wishes at any time, I realize now. For he is a shape-shifter of extraordinary talent, able to make of himself anything under heaven. As Uriel is, as Luc is, too.

As I was, I comprehend suddenly. And am no longer. I feel a stab of intense sadness at the thought.

"*Te gnovi,*" I gargle through the blood in my mouth. "I know you."

* * *

His touch is like living fire. It's almost enough to revive the dying. Almost. But Lela is marked for death, and even Gabriel cannot resurrect the dead. It is not within the compass of his powers.

He was my friend once. Like a brother. My protector and my champion. And I loved him dearly. The only ones more dear to me were Luc and . . . Raph, I remember with a start.

Instantly, Raph is standing in my mind's eye. The physician, the healer. With sable eyes and long dark hair, the color of obsidian. A strong, angular face with a mouth made for laughter and compassion. Skin of a pale ochre color, like desert sand, the burnished surface of an alien star. White raiment so blinding that its outline is indistinct. Like a living statue, a being of pure fire, youthful in aspect, yet ageless. Raph. How long has it been since I last saw him, touched him, too?

And then time seems to stand still. And everything with it. Save for Gabriel and me.

"I warned you," Gabriel says. "I warned you, but you would not listen, and now you see what transpires when human emotions are allowed full rein. Jealousy, violence, rage, death. Why will you not stay your hand, as we have counseled you repeatedly? Why must you always act? With heart foremost and not mind? *Be* as we are supposed to be, *act* as we are supposed to act: *in*humanly, not humanly; impartially, without 'empathy.' You have forgotten more than you know if you believe anything that happens down here even concerns you.

"Your beloved, Luc, is a liar," he continues, as I look upon his countenance with longing and regret. "Nothing he does, or directs you to do, is intended to be straightforward—you have drawn that human boy here for nothing but the purpose of sorrow. Agony, fear, complexity, misery, pain, and corruption, these are Luc's preferences in all dealings. You would do well to heed me now, as you never have in the past. Now more than ever, Luc seeks you, and you must not let yourself be found. *Everything* hinges on it. You have not been— how do these humans put it?—keeping your head down. *Do nothing*, Mercy. Just *survive*. That is the best we can hope to offer you."

"What if I wish to do more than *nothing*?" I cry. "Do more than merely . . . survive? How could you think that I'd be content to 'live' like this? I want *out*. Now. I've had enough. Life is about *choice*, remember?"

"It isn't possible." Gabriel's voice is regretful. "If absolute freedom were restored to you, the outcome could not be guaranteed. And it must be; everything hangs on it. I cannot say more on the subject. The less knowledge you have, the better. You were always . . . dangerous, unpredictable. As much as your paramour was and ever has been. And you've only grown more so. You're not supposed to be sentient. You're not supposed to overcome the obstacles we have placed in your way. That isn't part of the plan."

"I . . . don't . . . understand," I rasp.

Gabriel's smile is rueful. "You're not supposed to. It's a . . . miracle that we're even having this conversation. I didn't think I'd ever hear your voice again, in *any* lifetime, Mercy. Oh, and I *hear* you—it is undeniably you, despite the human shell you've been forced to assume. Uriel was right: beyond all understanding, despite all our safeguards, you're back."

"I'm not *back*," I snap, sudden anger choking my voice. "I'm like Frankenstein's monster; a golem set at the city gates, howling at the sky. Shambling, half alive."

Gabriel's tone grows unexpectedly gentle. "So much more than a mere *golem*, Mercy. Think of Lela, Jennifer,

Lauren, Lucy, Susannah, and Ezra before them—what great changes you have wrought in each life. You showed compassion for Justine, who has never been shown compassion by anyone, even herself."

"I liked Lela's life," I say. "It was so simple. Why couldn't you have just let me stay, grow old . . . ?"

Go with Ryan, I finish, for my ears alone.

Gabriel's voice turns harsh. "Raphael is the architect of this plan; raise your complaints with him. I argued against it from the start. To go from absolute, unmitigated freedom to . . . to . . ." His arms tighten about me. "I would rather have been put to the sword than endure what you have. It was not possible for you to remain in one place for too long. We had to move you; to keep moving you. Could not leave you as Ezra, as Becky, as Yael, Menna, Saraswati, any of that legion we have been forced to use—all good, blameless lives. Knowing what you're like, what you're capable of, Luc would still have found you. The only other option was to have you bring Luc in on your own, and either let us deal with him or have you slay him yourself. You were fully justified in doing so, but you considered it the ultimate betrayal."

Slay him? Slay Luc? Ultimate betrayal? What did

Luc do to justify *death* at my hands? I love him, would
never wish him harm. There is that ache again when I
think of us, in our place, the whole world wished away,
the whole world we two, and we two alone.

"Even after everything Luc's done to you," Gabriel
continues, "you were too . . . wounded, too numb, to
understand which was the best course, let alone raise
your hand against him. It took a millennium just for us
to find you, then another for you to properly heal."

Gabriel and Uriel might believe me to be "back,"
but there's still a blank dark sea at the core of my memory that refuses to yield up its secrets.

"Though you've proved you're good at betrayal,"
Gabriel adds without bitterness or explanation. "No, on
balance, this has probably been a more than fitting pun-
ishment. Free will comes at a price. You've been forced
to learn over and over again what it means to have none,
which must be especially . . . testing in your case."

A stinging anger rises in me that we are debating
questions of philosophy while Lela Neill lies dying.

"You're wrong," I say. "Uriel, too. Humans exercise
free will every moment of their waking lives. How do
you think Ranald died? He *chose* to kill himself, which

has to be the ultimate expression of one's free will—the freedom to destroy oneself."

Gabriel laughs mirthlessly. "Uriel did mention your views hadn't changed; had only . . . radicalized. People like Ranald are expendable fodder—easily constrained, easily derailed. Any of our order, any of Luc's, from highest to lowest, may command them. They are spoilage and excess, weakness and vice, irredeemable, unrepentant, low, worthless. Eventually, that which defines them devours them. If there is any free will there—and I don't believe it for a second; they were never made in *our* image—it is the will to have one's will enslaved. To cede control. That is hardly what I would term *free*." He almost spits. "Love life? Revere it? They are no better than wild animals."

"When I knew you," I say in confusion, "you were not so . . ."

"Harsh?" Gabriel's laughter sounds forced. "I've observed and reflected upon humankind . . . oh, it seems like time without end. All the terrible wrongs they perpetrate on themselves and on each other—their wanton moral blindness—make me question even my own purpose.

"But enough of this; it is time for you to *go*. I can tell from your face that you know exactly what I mean. It is no longer wise for you to remain here. Any thought you had of 'saving' this one, you may set aside. Forget her. Forget any of these flawed vessels we procure for you."

"Cut me loose," I plead, not believing for a second that he'll do it.

Gabriel's voice is weary, tender. "You know I cannot do it. Do not ask it of me."

Uriel had said the same thing to me when I was Carmen Zappacosta.

"You were always good at toeing the party line," I reply bitterly.

"And you turned from us and condemned yourself," Gabriel snaps. "You think we have little better to do than to keep you *safe*?"

I feel the air between us begin to supercharge with energy, to burn like dry tinder.

"Don't make me angry, Mercy," he warns. "You are in no position to win any arguments with me today."

"Prove it." The challenge in my voice only intensifies the lightning in his eyes. "Prove that the Eight have been behind my . . . condition all this time. You say I can't trust Luc? I can't trust *you*, either. If I believed you, if I could remember how the hell I got into this mess, then I wouldn't fight this . . . situation so hard. I'd find it easier to do . . . nothing. Let myself be blown from one place to another like the waves, like the clouds."

"Then believe this." Gabriel's voice is as the wind ghosting through ancient pines; like a storm building rapidly over the ocean. "For it is as Uriel told you. It has always been for you, *always*. This is how it was for you, and how it can never be again. Believe it and *mourn*."

21

In that instant, Gabriel collapses into a towering cloud of fine silver mist above me, swirling and dense, taking all the heat with it. As I fall to the floor, I look up into the lightning at the heart of that cloud, and it falls upon me like a rain of mercury, a rain of fire, and engulfs Lela, me, us.

Consumes us. Becomes us. Three into one.

Gabriel moves *through me*—like a swarm of raging locusts—and I feel, as I did in my dream of Ryan, our separate strands, all there. We are wholly distinct, although somehow loosely contained together in the one vessel. Lela is in there, like a locked box, a closed circuit, her soul so twisted and hooked in deep that I can't find a way to break through to her. She can't free herself; she can't slip the knot. And there *is* a knot, I'm certain of it.

I can feel us—her and me—*anchored* inside her body by bonds no human being could hope to sunder.

The pressure builds and I feel every cell, every nerve ending, in Lela's body convulse. There's a vast electrical storm inside us that is more potent than anything a mortal alone could withstand. It burns through the veil of time itself so that I see, I see—

Myself and Luc, a shining multitude at our backs, the Eight arrayed against us, holding their instruments of power aloft, a glimmering host behind Them, stretching farther than the eye can comprehend. It is what Uriel showed me before: the two of us the epicenter of something vast, a conflagration waiting to happen—but seen through Gabriel's eyes.

I feel a shock when I behold my golden beloved again, as if the moment is *now* and not some long-distant past that has already slipped through my fingers. Luc's beauty, his terrible power, is piercing, and when I see myself through the lens of Gabriel's gaze, my left hand grasped tightly in Luc's right—so tall, pale, and luminous, the two of us, even among that shining throng—I know that in that moment I was invincible because I was under Luc's protection.

For he was the highest ranked of them all, whispers

a small voice inside. *Or so he claimed for himself.*

Luc and me, proof against all the world.

What happened to us?

Then I see a steep distant mountainside—in Greece? Tibet? Russia?—inaccessible to all, save the most foolhardy; the soil scorched for leagues around, every tree, plant, animal, and rock in the vicinity of the deadly crater upon one lonely slope utterly destroyed, reduced to ashes.

I see Gabriel combing souks, markets, fairs, uprisings, gatherings of every form and description in a thousand cities that will never live again. In search of something, someone—*me*? I sense his frustration, his growing anger, how he almost tears down the physical world in his search—leaving in his wake unnatural storms and weather patterns, random lightning strikes that devastate all. Like me, he is not always the most . . . even-tempered.

Then he takes us into a series of chambers deep beneath the streets of an ancient human city. It is a place truly out of a nightmare: both crypt and ossuary, piled high with centuries of the dead. Walls, floors, ceilings, all carpeted with bones—grinning skulls, femurs, tibias, pelvic girdles; full skeletons arranged in grisly tableaux; everywhere the bodies of the ancient dead laid out on marble tombs, arranged in sepulchres in the seeping walls. The smell of decay, mildew, waste, the dust of ages, is thick in the air, which is itself alive with the sounds of running water, of rats and mice, of creeping, chitinous life.

In this hellish domain stand seven men, unnaturally tall, preternaturally beautiful, youthful, unmarked, ageless, each like a beacon, a lighthouse, unto himself. They have no need for external illumination, for each is a being of pure fire, casting no shadow.

They are gathered about a stone table, discussing in low voices the remains laid out upon it. Only one is missing from their number: flame-haired, emerald-eyed Gabriel, who steps now into this chamber, which is the last in a series of echoing rooms so deep within the earth that mortal man has surely forgotten them.

"Brother, well met," says the being I knew as Jeremiel, silver-eyed, auburn-haired, with a voice like exaltation. It sends a shiver through me to see him again, to hear him, though the words he speaks are already dust and memory.

I see Uriel there, too, one eyebrow raised sardonically as he says, "You took your time, brother."

Gabriel ignores him, asks of Jeremiel eagerly, "Can you be certain . . . ?"

In answer, the circle of men—of creatures more than man—part to allow Gabriel into their midst. What I see on that marble dais—twisted, blackened, shrunken—brings a ringing scream to Lela's blue-tinged lips, which wrenches me out of memory into the present.

And I see that my left hand is afire, the flames fully visible though it is daylight.

I hold my burning fingers up to my face, and my cries of anguish echo off the walls of the Green Lantern, breaking against the still forms of the humans that surround me. I feel the heat of the flames bleed into the air, but the pain is only a ghostly trace of the original agony that once almost consumed me. Of that agony I felt when I woke to find Them standing over me, judgment in Their eyes, every one of Them, all those years ago.

Where did the time go? Where was Luc when I begged Them to put me out of my misery in that grim realm of the dead and They denied me? Forced me to *live.*

The full horror of that memory, of what I was reduced to, assails me again, and I cannot speak the words, though I think them. *Why didn't you do it? Why didn't you put me down like a dog?*

As if in answer, I feel Gabriel surge through Lela's dying frame, as though he has become reduced to his base particles, a storm front of liquid fire, of inexorable energy. He leaves no physical mark of his passing, but, just like that, he has eaten away at the foundations of my absolute, unshakeable faith in Luc, and now there is doubt there, in my gaze, where before there was none.

Who lies to me? Who lies?

He leaves us and coalesces rapidly into his human form. I take a great heaving breath, coughing and gasping, no longer racked by the torment of spiritual possession.

The being that is Gabriel gently lifts me into his arms. "So you see," he utters sorrowfully, "how easy it was to carry you out of that place and devise a means of hiding you inside a vast array of human lives over many, many years. You were nearly spent when Selaphiel located you. While it is true that we want to keep you and Luc apart, it is not true that we wish you . . . dead.

We were simply forced to find a means of shielding you from Luc's attention, of throwing him off your trail. He was looking for you in all the places we had been, and we have only managed to stay ahead of him because we Eight united in this purpose almost as soon as you were . . . lost to us."

Is that pain in his gaze, I wonder. Why would he have cared if I was lost? Why must Luc and I—star-crossed lovers, if ever such a thing existed—be kept apart?

Gabriel frowns. "The only flaw in Raphael's plan has been that strange continuing connection you have with Luc—as if he marked you in some way that cannot be seen by any, save him. It is especially strong when you are asleep, when the linkages between mind and body are at their weakest. When you are at rest, he has access to your thoughts and pursues you across all the hours of darkness, only to have that connection snatched away at daybreak."

Gabriel's tone grows graver still. "It is time. If Michael knew I'd given you even this much insight into your . . . condition, he would not be pleased."

I recall Michael, and how he is, terrible in his beauty and his wisdom. I am sure he has not changed in all this time. To him, change is something that occurs only within established and permissible parameters: the seasons may change, the tides, the cycles of the moon and of the sun, but little else in nature. He is warlike, constant, always correct, dealing only in absolutes of black and white, admitting of no gray. Sometime in the dim past of our history together, he turned from me—or did I turn from him? Since that day, what lies between us has been an ocean of misunderstanding and rue.

Gabriel closes his brilliant green eyes, and I know I am about to leave this place, this third-rate café, and by no conventional means. He will cast me out into the vast sea of human souls, perform the strange necromancy that the Eight devised all those aeons ago. But I'm not sure I'm ready to go.

Ryan? I plead, all my longing in that word.

Not for you, Gabriel replies, without missing a beat, without opening his eyes. *Not your fate.*

Time recommences, and I hear Justine's terrified gasp.

"Of course you know him!" she cries. "Don't try to speak, Lela. Please. Oh God, oh God."

"Stand aside, sir," says a male voice beside us.

Sulaiman only holds me more tightly to him.

I feel Lela's body begin to convulse in his arms, blood pouring from her mouth. I am blind again. Cold and growing colder.

What happens now? I cry into the stillness between us.

It begins again, Gabriel sighs inside my mind. *And we will tell you to do nothing and you will do everything in your power to draw Luc to you, make ripples enough to signal to the universe that you yet live.*

I hear Cecilia and Justine wailing over Lela's body, while the paramedic tries to wrest her from Sulaiman's arms.

You know I will continue to defy you all, I reply. *And I shall do it again and again!*

No doubt. His voice is like a fleeting smile in my mind. *You have surprised us so far, we Eight; behaved more like us than your original self—the self we first cast into hiding. You had taken on all of Luc's worst traits—vanity, pride, self-indulgence, cruelty. But since you've been . . . banished*—when Gabriel says the word, his voice seems troubled—*you've taken so many souls out of Luc's grasp. Some of us argue that you have changed irreversibly; that the centuries-long game we have engaged in has changed you—for the better. Others of us are not so sure; we believe that were Luc to reclaim you tomorrow, you would be as you once were, save infinitely more powerful.*

Now you have forced our hand once more, he adds, a touch of anger in his tone. *And you must flee this broken body for a new home.*

His hold on me grows tighter, and I gurgle, "Wait!"

He grows still, tells the wailing women around us, "Quiet! Lela speaks."

I feel a surge of the living fire that Gabriel represents. Not enough to banish the mark of Azrael from Lela's body, but enough to enable *me* to be understood, to undertake one last accounting of my own.

The humans grow still, strain forward to hear my words, spoken through pain, through blood, through the harsh susurration of my breathing.

"Justine, promise me you'll place a higher value on yourself. Never sell yourself short again. Promise."

She nods tearfully. "I p-promise," she stutters, clutching one of Lela's cold hands in hers. "You hear me? It's a deal."

"Franklin?"

I can't see him through Lela's sightless eyes, but I hear him clear his throat gruffly, mumble, "Yes?"

"Tell your wife everything. Cause and effect, Franklin. Let your cowardice haunt you all the rest of your days, because this is partly your doing. . . ."

For a second, I grip Justine's hand fiercely in mine. "And find Ryan. Tell him . . . that Mercy shall come again. . . ."

Lela's voice trails away as her lungs fill up with blood. Gabriel loosens his hold on me, and I feel Lela's eyes roll back in her head as I cede control of her dying mind, her soul still knotted tightly into the wreckage of her body.

I'm so sorry, Lela.

Cecilia and Justine wail and wail. It's a primal sound, the grieving ululation of women everywhere. I could be in the Hebron, Uzbekistan, Bangladesh, Haiti, Rwanda, Kandahar, Jiangxi, the Sudan. Grief is universal. It transcends language, even time. And it is always the women who are left to grieve.

Though this time, there is one other to join their grieving number. And I pray he will receive and understand my message.

There is a sensation, a tug, as if Gabriel has broken some kind of cord that binds me to Lela. I am like beads on a broken string, each being drawn slowly upward and pocketed. I feel myself become something like mist, like fog, the bonds between myself and Lela's body beginning to loosen.

Inside Gabriel's mind I cry: *Command Azrael to reap them gently. Command him to lead Lela's soul, the soul of her mother, home. . . .*

Home.

Where the great universe wheels and turns and turns. Where planets and stars, suns and moons, the greater and lesser bodies, fly by; strange fissures in time and space twist and curl overhead like a painted, yet living, ever-changing dome. A place I have not seen for millennia, but to which I hope one day to return, to see again with waking eyes.

Mercy, Gabriel says, for my ears alone. *It is a good name you have given yourself; an apt name.*

Godspeed, I hear him murmur before I find myself falling out of this life, into another. . . .

ACKNOWLEDGMENTS

Of course, this book wouldn't have been possible without the love and support of Michael, Oscar, Leni, and Yve.

Thanks also to Lisa Berryman, Rachel Denwood, Carla Alonzi, Natalie Costa Bir, Elizabeth Ryley, and Nicola O'Shea for their expertise, professionalism, wisdom, and good humor; and to Cristina Cappelluto, Shona Martyn, and Evangeline for believing there was something to Mercy in the first place.

To Chris O'Connor of the Primitive Radio Gods— thank you for the music. And the words.

Thanks to the marvelous Catherine Onder, Hayley Wagreich, and Stephanie Lurie at Disney-Hyperion and to my excellent editorial and publishing team at Ravensburger Buchverlag.

Thanks also to Libby Callinan for tips on grammar, Shakespeare, and quiche over the years.

And *gratias ago*, Norma Pilling, for giving Mercy more facility with Latin than she is entitled to have, and for pointing out stubborn instances of the Toorak nominative.